BILL THESKEN

Books by Bill Thesken

The Lords of Xibalba
The Oil Eater
Blocking Paris
Edge of the Pit
The Catalina Cabal

BILL THESKEN

ISBN 978-0-9903519-9-3
ISBN 978-1-7329689-0-5

Behold, the Lord is emptying the earth and laying it bare. He is distorting its surface and scattering its inhabitants.

Isaiah

1.

"I'm sorry," she said. "We can still be friends."

He bent forward from the force of the sucker punch to his gut and struggled to catch his breath. He held the cell phone tight to his ear, nearly breaking it with his white knuckle death grip.

"I'm really sorry, Bob," she said again, this time with an emphasis on the word really.

"You're a *really* nice guy." She put a hopeful tune into her voice to placate him. "I know you'll find someone else."

"Sara, please…"

The phone went click and that was that. A few moments went by before he remembered to breathe again, a shallow inhale followed by a long lonely sigh as he pressed his forehead against the window pane for support.

She broke up with him over the phone. After five months. A phone call. He looked out the window at the grey morning fog hanging over the city like a cold, wet blanket before sitting down in his leather chair with a low thump. Eight o'clock on a Monday morning at the end of summer, and here he was starting the day, and the week, and the rest of his life, with a sledgehammer to the midsection.

She wouldn't even let him get a single word in edgewise, he didn't have time to tell her about the trip he planned to Tahoe.

The cabin, the hiking, swimming in the cool mountain streams, watching the stars roll overhead while sitting next to the campfire. All the things she liked to do, far away from the noise and distractions of the city.

He didn't actually have reservations for a cabin, or had even looked for one, but he was planning on taking care of all of those pesky little details during the week and then surprising her on Friday night.

He'd been working too much and not paying attention to the little things. He should have seen the warning signs sooner, and acted faster. But his boss was a slave driver, chaining him to this desk all day plus nights and weekends. All work and no play makes Bobby a bachelor.

He'd made it through a draining divorce two years ago, and finally after all those heart wrenching lonely days and nights, he thought he'd found someone to share his life with again. Someone vibrant and free-spirited and alive. With stunning legs and beautiful eyes.

"I'll call her back," he thought. "Reason with her,

and tell her all about the wonderful adventures I have planned." He smiled with a sudden vision of her running through a field of yellow flowers and leaping joyfully into his arms. He pressed his phone to activate it, then ever so gently touched her little pixie face on his contact list and waited for her to answer.

CALL BLOCKED, the screen displayed in big bold red letters.

After his ex-wife dumped him a few years ago, filed a restraining order against him, ran up the credit cards past the debt limit, and wouldn't answer his calls, Bob downloaded an app to his phone that could tell if his dialed calls to her weren't just being ignored, but were actually being blocked. He'd forgotten that he even had the app till this very moment, and hadn't seen those two dreaded words in a long time.

He shook his head in dismay. Not again.

"Hey," he said, snapping his fingers.

'Maybe the link on my phone is corrupt,' he thought. 'I'll dial manually this time.' He pulled up the keypad on the screen and punched in her ten digit number.

CALL BLOCKED.

He dialed again, extra slow this time to make sure he got each and every number right.

CALL BLOCKED.

It hadn't taken very long for her to start blocking his calls.

As his heart sank into his obliterated frame, he reached across his desk and turned the small picture frame with the smiling pixie face upside down, then slid it slowly across the desk, over the edge, and into the trash can.

"Now what am I going to do?" he wondered out loud. Thirty-five years old and time was running out. His options were dwindling.

There was a light knock on the half-opened door to his office then a grim face peered in at him. It was Ellie, the secretary who answered the phones for everyone on the floor. She wasted no words.

"Boss wants to see you."

Bob nodded. "Great."

The report was due last Friday, but he talked the boss into giving him the weekend to complete it. A statistical analysis of the habits of car buyers. They needed it for the presentation to the stockholders of the company on Wednesday. The boss wasn't very happy with his request.

"You're putting us into a bind," said the boss.

"I want to make sure the numbers are correct," Bob countered. "Statistics are fragile. You have to be careful with the final presentation."

The boss narrowed his eyes and pointed his finger at him. "Have it first thing Monday morning."

And here it was. A wonderful grey bastard of a Monday morning. He picked up the manila folder with the three printed copies of the report, his laptop, and the data stick with the digital presentation. He headed through the thick door, down the hall, past cubicle after cubicle to the end of the hall that opened up into a virtual courtyard of fountains and plants, and a stone-faced secretary guarding the entrance like an arch-angel guarding the gates of Heaven with a flaming sword. In all the time he'd worked there, Bob had never seen her smile, and at times he wondered if she was in fact a robot. But he discounted that as impossible. At least with a robot you could program a smile once in a while.

"They're waiting for you," she said without a single trace of humanity.

He nodded politely to her, focusing not on her lack of civility, but instead on the enormous task at hand, the big presentation that had taken a large chuck of his time, and cost him a relationship.

He opened the door and walked into the ornate dark cherry wood paneled office with the giant oak desk topped with marble. The boss was sitting with his animated hands gesticulating wildly in front of him, telling a story that ended with a bang of his hand on the marble. The two other people sitting in front of him laughed at the punchline.

Bob smiled and walked further into the room. "Hello everyone."

As they turned, their happy smiles melted into frowns, perturbed at the interruption of their little moment of levity by the mundane necessity of business.

The boss stood while the others did the same. "Bob, you know Carl from accounting and this is Woodward from corporate."

Woodward, *what the hell kind of a puffed up stuffy name is that*, thought Bob as he wrinkled his brow. He figured, what the heck, might as well join in the fun. He's just another one of the guys, and he might as well lighten everyone's suddenly sour mood with a joke.

"Is your nickname Woody?"

The answer was quick and severe, and his frown deepened. It was almost as though a bucket of ice cold water had been poured on top of his head. "It's Woodward."

"Oh, sorry."

"I actually hate the name Woody. It reminds me of someone with no brains."

The boss was abrupt. "Woodward is our new vice president, he graduated from Yale just last year. He also has a degree from Harvard, if you can imagine that."

Actually Bob could not imagine that, and yet nodded while making a note to himself to never again make the mistake of venturing a nickname for someone he'd just met. Especially someone who graduated from an Ivy League school.

"Is that our report?" asked the boss.

Bob was beaming, and happy to change the subject. "Why yes it is."

"Well, let's get on with it."

Bob handed out the separate printed copies to the three men, then plugged the data stick into his laptop computer portal, pointed the projector lens at the wall and when the screen lit up, he began his presentation, scrolling through page after page of data, graphs, and numbers. It was an utterly boring report, but for a statistician it was thoroughly concise, in effect a 3-D view of the many varied buying habits of automotive consumers.

When he was finished, the boss and Carl from accounting looked rather pleased, while the Yale/Harvard graduate looked puzzled. He flipped through the pages with narrowed eyes while shaking his head ever so slightly.

"How long did this report take to produce?" asked Woodward. He was now looking directly at Bob, who started to sweat under his collar.

"A little under three weeks."

"Hours. How many hours."

Bob thought hard to himself. What the hell, I don't have a timeclock in my office pal, how the heck should I know how many hours? *Don't make it seem too long*, he thought, *or they'll think you're a dumb ass. Plus I shouldn't make it too short or they'll think I skimped on my work.*

"About two hundred hours," answered Bob.

"You see?" said Woodward, turning to the boss. "It's a waste of man hours. Two hundred hours for a task that would take our new software program less than a millisecond to compute."

"But you have to input the data," said Bob. "That's where the real time comes in."

"I can teach a monkey to input data," replied

Woodward as he slowly turned back around. And the look in his eyes told Bob that his little crack about how his nickname should be Woody was still resonating, and not in a good way.

Woodward looked at his watch then picked up the report, placed it in his briefcase and clicked the latches closed. "Well, I have a plane to catch, thank you all for the briefing." He reached over and shook the boss's hand, and Carl's from accounting, but did not offer his hand to Bob. He picked up the handle of the briefcase with his right hand while smoothing his hair with his left. "Good luck," he said to Bob and headed for the door.

For some odd reason, Bob didn't think he really meant good luck.

"I'll walk you out," said the boss while hurrying around his desk and shadowing Woodward to the foyer.

"Well, I'd better get back to my office," said Carl.

At least *he* had the decency to reach over and shake Bob's hand. "It was a thorough presentation. I thought it was quite well researched." When he could see that the boss and Woodward had left the room and were out of earshot he continued. "A lot of people don't understand the intricacies of what we do. Numbers scare them so they're intimidated by people who are experts with them. I'm probably telling you something you already know."

Bob had an anecdote. "You know the old saying, there's power in numbers."

Carl smiled. "Sure, if you're in an Army at war on the battlefield then yes, strength of numbers can be a determining factor in victory or defeat. Unfortunately for us, accountants and statisticians are never placed on the pedestal, and I'm afraid you might have ruffled young Woodward's feathers. His father, by the way, is a majority shareholder in the company. That's how he got to be a vice president."

"You mean he didn't get the job with his two degrees?"

"You can buy just about anything with money these days. Or maybe it's always been that way. Anyways, good to see you again Bob, I'm off to the trenches. Good luck."

This time, Bob knew the offer of good luck was genuine. Carl turned and walked away through the door.

That's the second time someone told me good luck in the past few minutes, thought Bob. Usually telling someone good luck turns the other way around into bad luck, that's why you never tell someone good luck when they're going fishing. Whenever the cast in a play is heading out onto stage, you never tell them good luck, you tell them all to break a leg. If you really want them to have good luck, you tell them to break both legs.

The boss came back through the door and went around the desk and sat down again while Bob shut down the computer and pulled out the data stick.

"Why don't you have a seat for a moment," said

the boss and motioned to one of the chairs in front of him.

Bob made sure to sit in the chair vacated by Carl. "Yes sir."

"Can I have the data stick?" he asked, and Bob handed it over to him. "Well I have some good news and some bad news."

Bob blinked, and his heart skipped a beat. Conversations like this usually never ended well.

"The good news first is that we're giving you a five thousand dollar bonus."

Happy days. Bob beamed at that, nearly splitting his lower lip with a giant smile that suddenly stretched from ear to ear.

It was short lived.

"The bad news is we're letting you go."

Punch to the gut. Bob tried to keep his composure while inside, he felt like he was taking a karate kick to his solar plexus and a bowling ball to his nuts. Breathe, man, breathe. Keep breathing he told himself, *don't ever let them see the fear in your eyes or you're a dead man.* But the smile on his face slackened like a limp rubber band.

"I don't understand."

"It's a corporate decision. Straight from the top. The company is downsizing some of our departments, we're streamlining, optimizing, upgrading systems to meet the demands of a new digital society."

Double talk.

"Is it because I called the owner's son Woody?"

"No, no, no of course not. That has nothing to do with it."

They would never admit to it, of course. Couldn't have a disgruntled ex-employee going after a corporate big-wig with an ax.

"So the bonus is my severance pay?"

"You might call it that."

"What about my vacation time? I have three weeks stored up."

"We're giving you an extra two weeks of vacation time, which is standard company policy for situations such as this, plus the three weeks you have stored up, and the bonus check. Five weeks of vacation, and five thousand dollars. That should help get you through the adjustment period to another job, which I hope you find right away. We'll give you a nice letter of recommendation. You can stop by accounting and they'll have your check ready for you."

Paying me off so I would go away quietly.

"How soon do you want me to leave?"

"Today."

Bob sighed, what a morning. First his girlfriend and now this.

"Well, I suppose I should go clear out my office."

"It's already been done."

"What?"

"Security is waiting for you downstairs at the front door of the lobby, and will escort you out of the building."

"What about my personal items? My plants and

pictures?"

"All boxed up and ready to go."

Bob thought about his ex-girlfriend's pixie-faced picture at the bottom of the trash can and shrugged. She was the one who gave him the plants, and now they were trash too.

Everything in his office was a pile of rubbish to him now. It was time to start over. He had his laptop in his hands, and his wallet, car keys and phone in his pocket. They could have everything else. He got up to leave, thought twice about it, then reached over the desk with the intent to shake the bosses hand. The simple gesture was not returned and the boss gave a little harrumph, turned around behind his desk, picked up a pile of folders, then set them down with a heavy thud on the marble top in front of him and started rummaging through them, ignoring the person in front of him. Without looking up he said: "Now if you don't mind I have a lot of work to do."

"Sure," said Bob, and ever so slowly pulled his empty hand back and turned for the door. "See you around."

He went out the heavy double doors, past the secretary, got in the elevator, and punched the button for the fifth floor: accounting.

Janet who was manning the front desk in payroll had his check ready for him and gingerly handed an envelope to him. She wore a sweet sympathetic face.

Bob opened up the packet and looked at the number. It said five thousand dollars, the exact amount of his severance pay. His eyes narrowed as he looked back up at Janet. "What about my vacation pay?"

She shook her head. "Vacation pay is considered a normal paycheck Bob, and it comes out every other Friday just like everyone else's. We can't cut it early." She grinned sheepishly, embarrassed for him. "I'm sorry, it's company policy."

The boss upstairs lied, he was only going to get the bonus check today. That slippery bastard. Bob reached over and put his hand on the front door knob to steady himself, the solid feel of the metal was reassuring, then he felt a sudden urge to tear the door off the hinges with his bare hands, and use it as a battering ram to destroy the accounting office until he got all the money owed to him. Completely demolish this office and then head up to the boss's office and do the same. Then he'd strap the liar to the door and sail it out the window.

But security was waiting to escort him out of the building, and they were probably at the boss's office also as a precaution.

Bob took a deep breath, letting it out slowly like steam from a boiling kettle, and just like that, the anger passed. After all, Janet was just a worker bee in the big hive, doing her job, as were all the other people in the office, workers in a hive, just like Bob was a few minutes ago, so he didn't argue. He'd already been dumped and fired, no need to put arrested on his resume for the day.

"I have direct deposit you know."

She nodded, with a forced smile that looked painful. She just wanted Bob to leave. "It'll be in your account first thing Friday morning. I promise."

Bob nodded and looked longingly at the accounting office in the background. Row upon row of busy desks filled with happily employed people. Not even one little space for a statistician.

I've hit rock bottom, he thought then turned on his heels and walked out of the room. Bypassing the elevator doors, he chose instead the stairwell, taking the metal steps down to the first floor to clear his mind. *I don't deserve to take the easy way down in an elevator. I'm a loser.*

2.

Outside, the cold fog washed over his face, a kiss of wet mist that nearly refreshed him, almost bringing a smile to his face.

Almost.

He remained stone cold sober. There was no reason to be happy. He'd just been tossed to the sidewalk like a sack of garbage.

The concrete parking garage was set across the four lane street and he waited at the light with a dozen other people to cross. His pre-paid designated parking space that went with his employment was on the first floor, tenth from the entrance. He could see the little blue sedan parked facing out, ready for a quick exit.

A tow truck was backing through the garage, it's warning beep echoing out onto the street irritating everyone in earshot, backing up right in front of his little blue sedan.

"What the heck…" muttered Bob.

Two burly men got out of the tow truck and

headed to the rear and began to hook up the blue car. Bob stood on the sidewalk as if in a dream, a deer in the headlights as they finished hooking up the bumper, one of the burly men on the side pulled a lever, and the front of the little blue car lifted up. Bob reached over and punched the cross walk button repeatedly.

"C'mon, c'mon."

"That doesn't work you know," said an old woman standing next to him. "It might even jam the mechanism."

Bob ignored her and considered running across the busy street and taking his chances avoiding the oncoming traffic, and then dismissed the idea.

"With the luck I'm having today I'll be squashed like a bug on someone's windshield."

The burly men finished their bastardly deed and were getting back into the tow truck when the little man in the cross-walk box turned green. Bob was like an Olympic sprinter at the starters' gate and made it across the street in just a few leaps, getting to the parking exit just as the tow truck was about to leave. He ran right up to the front of the tow truck and blocked it, waving his hands in the air.

"Wait! Stop! That's my car you have there!"

The burly guy in the driver's side frowned and got out with a folded piece of paper in his hand. He'd been through this song and dance before. He opened the papers to read the contents.

"You Bob Tauber?"

"Yes, yes. And that's my car."

"You're late on your payments, the car is being re-possessed by the bank, we have full authorization to remove it, here's my ID." The burly man showed him a laminated card.

"Yes, I know I'm a little late on some payments, I thought I had an agreement with the bank."

"Didn't you get the letter they mailed you?"

"What letter?"

"The letter saying they were going to take the car back unless you brought your payments up to date."

"Maybe I missed that one." He was being bled dry by his ex-wife and the alimony payments, while trying to impress his new—but now—ex-girlfriend with gifts and dinners, on his puny (now extinct) paycheck, not to mention the apartment rent that was also overdue.

"Look pal, I have a schedule to keep. I have to get this vehicle back to the storage lot, and get on to the next repo before lunch. I don't have time for any shenanigans."

Bob thought hard, and then hit his forehead with his hand. The bonus check. He shouted out. "I have money! I just now received a check that I can cash at the bank and get my payments up to date! Please." Bob begged. "I just lost my job and my girlfriend, it's been a tough morning."

Cars were trying to get in and out of the parking garage honking their horns, but the burly guy remained stoic, and waved them around, then looked down at the paper.

"Alright, it says here that you are behind ten payments at four hundred per month, that's four thousand dollars, plus the current payment of four hundred. Really pal? You haven't paid in almost a year? You want me to get you a calculator? The total you owe the bank today is four thousand four hundred dollars. Plus my fee of three hundred. Forty seven hundred clams buddy. You pay that today and we let you keep the car. Otherwise step aside, before I call my pal Morris here out of the truck. And I don't want to hear any more whining about your job or your girl."

Bob looked over at the burly guy's partner who was sitting straighter in his seat now, glaring through the windshield, agitated, eyes flaring, gritting his teeth while chewing on the end of a well-worn cigar. He certainly didn't look like a Morris. More like a Brutus, or Attila.

"I have right here in my pocket a paycheck for five thousand dollars."

"Let's see it, and a driver's license for ID."

Bob pulled out his wallet with his license and the bonus check and handed them over for inspection.

The burly repo man held the documents in his beefy hands, squinted at them for a moment, then shook his head while letting out a growling sigh. "I must be getting soft." He handed them back and studied Bob while rubbing the black stubble on his chin.

Finally, he made up his mind and nodded. "This

must be your lucky day pal," as he waved to the truck. "Alright, jump in and we'll take you to the bank down this road. You go inside and clear up your payments and we'll give you back your car. But I don't want this taking too long. You got fifteen minutes from when we get to the bank to get this taken care of. You can't get it done by then we're out of there, you got that?"

Bob squeezed in the truck and the burly guys partner reluctantly moved to the middle. Bob held out his hand for a shake, but was ignored.

It was probably all for the best, since the enforcer had hands covered in what looked like a mixture of road tar and axle grease and an aroma that said he hadn't taken a shower in a few months, maybe years.

Still, Bob was happy to have a chance to keep his car, and he remembered an old saying from the priest at his church when he was young; 'some of the happiest people in the world come home smelling to high heaven'.

If that old saying was true Bob thought, then the guy sitting next to him must be one of the happiest people on the planet.

In one hand and out the other, it was very easy to cash the check and make the payment, too easy in fact, and now he had a measly three hundred dollars remaining to his name until Friday.

He handed three crisp bills with Benjamin Franklin's face on them to the burley tow truck driver who carefully studied each one of them, then folded the bills into his front pocket as the enforcer unhooked the car.

"Well that was easy," said the re-po man. "Maybe your luck's about to change."

3.

Bob drove across town to his apartment, parked on the street in front of a red brick apartment building and slowly climbed the cement stairs, still reeling from the morning events.

Tacked on the front door was a hard red cardboard sign and stamped at the top in bold black letters: 'EVICTION NOTICE', while below in fine handwritten print the explanation: 'You are hereby given notice to vacate these premises for failure to pay the required rent.'

"What the hell," said Bob. "Is this even legal?"

He tried his key and, of course, it would not work.

"You can't just evict me with one day's notice, it's against the law." He muttered as he pulled out his phone and dialed his landlord.

"Well, well, well," said the voice on the other end. "If it isn't the elusive Bob Tauber. How can I help you?"

"Drew, you can't just evict me from my house."

"I'm afraid you're wrong about that."

"Aren't there laws to protect me? I thought you had to give me sixty days' notice."

"Listen deadbeat, you haven't paid your rent in over sixty days. It seems to me that you're the one that gave notice."

"Well, I've been a little short with money lately, but I'll have a paycheck on Friday, and I can pay you then."

"Pay me now and I'll let you back in."

"I'm telling you, it's against the law, you can't do this to me, it's not right."

"Call a cop."

"Well, maybe I'll do just that."

The phone clicked on the other end as Drew hung up.

"Yeah, that's what I'll do, I'll call the cops," Bob muttered then sat down on the cold, damp steps feeling utterly defeated, knowing that he would never do something like that, and he felt guilty for not paying his rent on time.

He sat on the steps outside the apartment building, and looked down the street towards the plaza on the corner. There was a convenience store, a laundromat, a pawn shop and a bar. Hanging high over the door of the bar was a little martini glass made out of fluorescent green tubes that lit up every two seconds.

He shook his disgusted head. "My girlfriend dumped me, I got fired from my job, the repo guy took most of my cash, and I got evicted from my apartment. But I still have three hundred dollars in my pocket." He sighed mightily, slumped to his feet and walked slowly towards the bar. "I guess this is what people normally do in situations like this."

It was dingy and dark with sawdust on the floor and it took a few minutes till his eyes got adjusted to the light. He sat at the end of the empty bar and waited for the bartender to make his way over. The clock on the wall read ten AM.

"Am I your first customer of the day?" Bob asked, hoping for a cheerful reply.

"Why yes you are," said the surly bartender. "And for that you win the grand prize." He set a bowl of mixed salty nuts and crackers in front of Bob. "What'll it be?"

"I guess just a beer." Then he thought twice about it. "And a shot of whiskey. Might as well live it up."

The front door opened and the dull light of day shone through for a moment and an old lady being led by a small scruffy poodle dog came through the entrance.

"You let dogs in here?" asked Bob.

"Sure," said the bartender. "Dogs, cats, horses, it's the new law in our wonderful city. Anyone can bring whatever animal they want into an establishment as long as it's a 'service animal' companion, and we can't even ask if it's a legitimate service animal, that violates their rights. They help the person cope with their 'feelings' and if we deny them entry we're denying them the basic right to health and happiness. One time a guy brought in a full grown hog and there was nothing we could do about it."

"What about my rights if the dog pees on me."

"You're out of luck pal, he's got more rights than you." The bartender went to the other end of the bar to get the beer and the shot.

Bob looked under his feet for the dog. With the way his luck was going, the mangy mutt was probably lifting its leg at that very moment. But the coast was clear with no fur was in sight. He relaxed when the bartender returned with a wide frosty mug and a little shot glass filled with a dark amber liquid. He could almost feel his blood pressure go down at the sight of it.

"To your health," said Bob as he gulped the entire shot of fire water with a grimace, then took a sip of the beer to cool it off.

A warm glow began to trickle, then flow throughout his body starting from the very top of his forehead and spreading far and wide along the length of his limbs to the tips of his fingers and toes, and finally he half smiled.

Everything was going to be okay after all. He'd find another job, another apartment, and maybe if he was lucky another girlfriend. "Easy squeezy," he murmured.

Halfway through the beer, nature called and would not be denied, so he pushed away from the bar and looked around for the restroom, which he saw just to the right of the entrance.

What he didn't see was the mangy furry mutt laying on the floor next to his foot and when he took a step it was with his full weight right on the dog's paw. It let out a series of blood curdling yelps like it was being killed and limped across the floor towards the old woman who was running to its aid and stooped low to pick up the varmint and cuddle it protectively in her arms.

She rushed up to Bob and swung her purse at his head and connected with a loud thump on his ear. Bob fell back against the bar with a ringing in his head and the woman charged at him again, swinging the purse like a wrecking ball. Bob held out his hand to block it and the strap wrapped around his wrist. The old lady lost her balance and fell straight down on top of her head, and was knocked out cold.

The bartender rushed around the bar, knelt beside her, then looked up at Bob.

"Gee pal, you didn't have be that rough with her."

"Me? I didn't lay a hand on her!"

Ten minutes later the ambulance arrived, followed by the police and the next thing Bob knew he was handcuffed with his hands behind his back on the barstool wondering what the hell just happened. The ER guys loaded the old lady onto a gurney at floor level with the dog on her chest, and then brought it up to waist high level and rolled her out the front door. She was strapped in and moaning loudly so everyone on the block could hear her, while her dog whined along with her.

A small crowd formed outside the door and were peering in, trying to see the action, some of them tried to get in, but a cop was blocking the door. Two other cops were standing in front of Bob, all business.

"I didn't touch her I swear," said Bob.

"Tell it to the judge," said the cop with the single stripe and the chip on his shoulder.

"You gotta believe me. Bartender, you saw the whole thing right?"

"All I saw," said the bartender, "was you with your hand in the air, and her flying onto her head."

The cop with the grey hair and sergeant stripes was studying Bob. "Let's get this straight. You claim that you accidently stepped on her dog, and she rushed towards you and attacked you with her purse and fell of her own accord, her own fault."

"That's the truth."

"Did you try to catch her? Break her fall? She's seventy years old."

Old enough to know better, thought Bob, but he kept that thought to himself. "It happened so fast I didn't know what to do, I was just trying not to get clobbered by her purse again. Did you check what she had in there? Maybe a cinder block? A bowling ball?" Bob could feel his left eye swelling up and he blinked out a tear.

"Yeah, she caught you a good one," said the Sergeant. You're gonna get a black eye, I can guarantee it. Alright we've heard both sides, she said you attacked her and her dog, you said you didn't touch her, and the bartender's testimony is non-conclusive, but it doesn't look good for you."

"Don't you have video surveillance in here?" asked Bob.

The two cops looked at the bartender who shrugged his shoulders in reply.

"Of course, doesn't everyone these days?"

"Why the heck didn't you tell us that in the first place?" said the sergeant and turned to his partner. "Alright, you stay with him. And you," pointing to the bartender, "let's go take a look at that footage."

Like a referee in a football game going under the hood to review the call on the field, they headed to the back room and the replay booth.

Five minutes later they reappeared, the grim faced sergeant and the red-faced bartender.

"Alright, let him go," said the sergeant. "She attacked you alright. Seventy years old or not a guy's got a right to put up his hand to keep from getting mugged. Just like you said, you didn't touch her. You want to press charges sir?"

"No, I just want to go home." And then as he was getting un-cuffed, he remembered that he was locked out of his apartment, he couldn't go home. He told his landlord he would call a cop, and here he was with a whole squad spread out around him, just waiting for a new job, a new bad guy to put in chains. But he put that thought out of his mind. *I didn't pay my rent*, he thought. *I'm the bad guy.*

4.

With his hands shoved deep in his pockets Bob walked glumly out of the bar and down the long lonely street to his car, sat in the seat and looked at his face in the rear view mirror. His cheek bone was swollen and a red bruise circled his eye. He shook his head in disgust.

"I got beat up by a seventy-year-old lady."

A tiny movement caught his eye and he looked at the top of the steering wheel, at a little black ant that was traversing the top, heading to parts unknown. Now here finally is something that I have complete control over, thought Bob.

"I'm the master of your universe, little helpless ant. I can crush you."

He aimed carefully with one eye, hovered his big fat thumb above the tiny ant, timing the quick descent perfectly, and brought it down fast and furious right down next to it and waited for it to climb on. The ant backed up, turned around and went the other way, but Bob placed the thumb in front of it on the other side and he could see the little tentacles searching his skin, then it climbed up and onto the thumbnail. Bob got out of the car and went over to a bush, set his thumb against the bark of a branch and waited for the ant to scurry off.

"You've been evicted from my car," he said. "Now scram, get outta here." Then he looked up at the front door with the red cardboard eviction notice and slowly back at the ant. "We have a lot in common, you and me." Bob's heart sunk. "But to be honest, right now I feel a whole lot smaller than you."

The fog was beginning to lift and break apart with the heat of the mid-morning sun, as Bob got back in his car and sat still, thinking hard, afraid to make a move in case it somehow caused more trouble.

Dumped, fired, evicted, and beaten up. And it wasn't even noon. The worst part by far was being dumped by his girlfriend. Sure he could find a new job, a new apartment, could just look in the newspaper want ads, and find both of those, and the soon-to-be black eye would heal over in time. But he wasn't as sure about the girlfriend part. There was never a guarantee in that department. They were few and far between, and harder to find as the years went by.

The pit of his stomach right below his heart was still in freefall and sinking. The very worst thing in a man's life is when your woman loses faith in you. No guy would ever want to admit it in public, but without a woman's faith in you, what else was there?

There was only a void. Since the beginning of time there was one thing, and one thing only that has driven humanity forward; guys trying to impress the chicks.

It was a competition, and it started early. On the playground in kindergarten, and all through grade school, high school, college if you were lucky, then spilling out onto the battle fields of the work place. It wasn't really you against the other guys either, it was you against the girls. How to break through that impenetrable mysterious unknown whatever it was that made them seem otherworldly.

It was a battle to win their attention, their affection, and when successful, a sense of worth that couldn't be put into words, a validation coming from that ethereal being that physically looked somewhat like you but was so different mentally and spiritually that it might as well be a separate species.

But what if you lose that affection, that sense of worth from that beautiful creature that had been fought for and won?

Lose that and a guy was doomed.

Then it hit him.

This whole time ever since the very first day that he was on that playground in kindergarten and saw that first girl that he'd ever laid eyes on, he'd been acting like a little pet dog, chasing his tail around and jumping around on his hind legs to get attention from the master.   Rolling around on the ground and barking for a treat. Trying to be a good dog so he'd get a scratch under his chin, or a belly rub.

He shook his head in disgust while gritting his teeth. It was actually much worse than that.

At work he was like a circus animal, a bear riding a bicycle around in a circle with a silly hat and suspenders, while the crowd laughed. Or a trained seal flopping awkwardly around on his front flippers, then climbing up onto an empty barrel and balancing a ball on his nose at the circus master's command.

His whole life was a sham, as a statistician and a mathematician, he added it all up and the bottom line was that he was no more than a beggar for affection.

In that moment of thought clarity he made up his mind.

"I have to get out of here. Get far away. And fast."

He sat there mulling over his options. He could drive just about anywhere in the country with three hundred dollars in gas, and his hybrid car. Then he made up his mind for the second time in the past few minutes, nodding his head in complete agreement with himself.

"I'll go to Tahoe." He gritted his teeth and set his jaw square, grimacing in defiance at the world.

"I'll damn well finish something I set out to do today." He made a fist and slammed into the palm of his hand. "I said I was planning a trip there, and I will damned well go there come hell or high water. I'll show her. I'll show everyone." He looked at his eyes in the rear view mirror. "Even myself."

He started up the car, revved the engine twice, checked his side mirrors, rolled down the windows and merged into traffic. When he was up to speed with the other cars he let out a primal yell, an animal unleashed. Then, as he passed a cop giving out a ticket, he immediately sat straight in his seat again. The cop heard the yell and with a grim face looked around at all the cars passing by, but couldn't make out which one of the bastards yelled at him.

Careful Bob, he thought to himself, *you just got of one scrape, and if you recall, you had a shot of whisky and a beer and it's not even lunchtime. Don't get thrown in jail for a DUI.*

He drove slow and careful till he was well out of the city. The buzz of the booze had worn off and was replaced by anger, despondence, resentment, fear of the unknown, and rebelliousness, all in that order.

After a short while he found himself in the middle of an endless line of cars that was heading away from the city, hemmed in on all sides, like a lemming in the middle of the pack, heading for the cliff.

5.

Two hours later, and twenty miles outside of Sacramento, he saw an old abandoned road set in the middle of a forest of low scrub brush and tumbleweeds. He pulled off the freeway in the middle of nowhere and got out of his car to take a look and stretch his legs.

The old cracked asphalt double lane highway was set about a hundred yards from the freeway running parallel to it. A horizontal monolith to a bygone era.

This must be the old road, he thought. *Before it got too small for the traffic load and they replaced it.*

Round chaparral brush and man-high weeds of every shape and size, dry and brown and dull green, grew wild and close to the edges and in the cracks of the ancient road. There was a crude attempt at a gate to block it: wind and sun bleached, termite eaten two-by-fours set on the tops of rusted barrels. He reached over and with his pinky finger gently pushed one of the two-by-fours, and it fell to the ground with a dull clatter.

"Looks like the road's open," he whispered.

Off in the distance he could hear the dull roar of the freeway, the steady drone of cars whizzing by with the occasional big-rig truck lumbering along in a constant stream of metal and rubber.

Resentment at the morning's events boiled over in his chest, bypassing his brain and better senses. He got in the car, rolled past the downed gate, pointed the front end down the center of the road and stomped on the gas pedal, the engine roared, the tires squealed, and he burned rubber up and down the old road till he got it out of his system.

It was both thrilling and frightening. From a complete dead stop the car shook and squealed and roared, the rear end jumping around and within mere seconds it was up to seventy miles an hour on an old cracked asphalt road with weeds and chaparral whizzing past the windows. Finally, he got her slowed down by stomping on the anti-lock brakes, which resisted every attempt to skid, then he turned the car slowly around like a mini dragster getting ready for the next heat, the next race against his imaginary opponent, and stomped on the accelerator again. He did this over and over again, until most of the resentment of the morning had been driven out by fear, adrenaline, and the exhilaration of pure speed.

At the end of his last run, as he was slowing down by the gate, he spotted three pre-teen boys on bikes who were watching him from the side, drawn to the sound of the mad racer. They were hidden from sight, or so they thought, in the high chaparral. When he made eye contact with them, they scampered on their bikes and rode away as a fast as they could from the hell raiser in the blue car, pedaling as fast as they could while looking back now and again to make sure he wasn't getting ready to race after and run them over.

He rolled over the two-by-four gate, got out and replaced it on the rusted barrel, then checked his rear tires and compared them with the front ones. Half the tread was shredded from rear tires, and they were shiny in places from the spinning, but he could see none of the inner steel belts showing through. He shrugged his shoulders.

"What the heck", he said out loud. "Sometimes a guy's got to burn a little rubber." He drove back to the entrance of the freeway slowly merging into traffic, a lemming once again, following the bumper of the car in front of him to the unknown cliff in the distance.

Somewhere east of Donner Lake and west of Truckee on the outskirts of Tahoe he took a wrong turn and found himself on a deserted stretch of highway. By the time he realized he was lost, it was getting dark; the sun setting behind the high mountain peaks that surrounded the whole area.

He saw a sign that read 'Private Camping - Clean & Affordable'.

The only word that mattered was the last one:

affordable. Free would have been better, but you take what you can get. He pulled off the gravel road and onto a rocky trail that led to a barn with a sign on it. It simply said 'Office'. He got slowly out of the car and stretched his legs.

An old man limped out from the side of the barn, carrying a clipboard in one hand and a wooden cane in the other that he balanced his frail frame against as he walked out to the car and squinted at Bob.

"You're late," said the old man.

"What do you mean?"

"The hippy convention was last week."

Bob was polite, he needed a place to stay. "I don't understand what you're talking about sir."

"Don't call me sir, I ain't in the military and you ain't that much younger'n me."

He was a cranky old man in his early seventies. Bob figured and knew it wouldn't pay to get into a tussle with him. All he needed right now was a place to stay for the night.

"I'm sorry, just my poor upbringing I guess."

The old man got back on point. "Well, aint you here for the hippy convention?"

"Me?"

"Yeah, aint you a hippy?"

What the hell is this guy talking about, thought Bob. Then he caught a glimpse of his outline in the side mirror. He'd driven the whole way up here, two hundred miles up the mountain with all the windows open, sixty, seventy, sometimes eighty miles an hour, and in the process he'd turned into a wild man, his hair was a tangled twisted mop on top of his head, the collar of his shirt rattled and torn, he kicked off his shoes long ago outside the city, and was barefoot to boot, wiggling his toes in the dirt. *I guess I do look like a hippy*, he thought.

"No, I'm not a hippy, but I probably look like one right about now."

"Well you missed a real hullabaloo I'll tell you that."

"It was a big deal huh?"

"Oh yeah, the meditating, the chanting, the yoga, the candle light massages, the naked girls running around the river and through the woods, getting back to nature and what not."

Bob could see the glint in the old man's eyes as he reminisced about the what not. He really liked hippy conventions, apparently. Then he shook his grey head in mourning and sighed.

"Well, anyways it's ten bucks a night for the campsite, you've got a picnic table, a water hookup, showers and a barbecue pit. There's a stream, a hiking trail, and a fire pit in the center of the park. There's a couple of other families staying overnight scattered here and there, but other than them it'll be pretty quiet, I figure. We're in between seasons and it's fairly slow these days."

He could tell that the old man wished the hippies were still here, and so Bob decided to cheer him up.

"Is the convention coming back next year?"

The old eyes lit up, and he slapped his thigh and let out a holler. "You betcha! Even bigger than the one they had this year, or so they're sayin'."

Bob noticed a giant ten-foot high, thirty-foot wide pile of trash to the side of the barn and the old man followed his eyes.

"Yeah, well they sure do leave a heap of a mess, they come out to nature and leave it all behind so to speak. I've got to get a dump truck out here to haul it all away. It'll cost me a couple of hundred bucks."

Bob could see hats and pillows and blankets, broken tents and coolers, a couple of mattresses, clothes, a bra or two, and piles of paper and pamphlets.

"There's some bits and pieces of trash still scattered around the park here and there, it takes about a week to clean up after them, they turn into wild animals in some ways, that's the downside of the whole event."

"Is it okay if I just stay the night?" asked Bob. "Maybe I'll stay longer, I don't know, I'm kind of on a loose schedule right now."

The old man nodded. "Sure."

Bob handed him a ten-dollar bill.

He drove past the barn and around the fire pit to the opposite side of the campsite and found a side road that led to an empty spot out of sight from the other families. He parked next to the picnic table.

"Home sweet home."

It looked like it was the farthest spot away from the barn and had not yet been cleaned of the trash from the last campers. But it wasn't too bad. The trash can was only half-full and had a lid on it and he checked to make sure it wasn't full of nasty smelly maggot filled food leftovers.

There was a pile of pamphlets and papers on the picnic table and a long silk something hanging from a low branch on the pine tree next to the faucet. He pulled it off and looked closely. It was purple with patterns etched into the surface, squares and rectangles and circles giving it the look of something a magician might use to make an pretty assistant or fluffy bunny disappear. He decided that it was a full length body wrap, some sort of a dress, fairly expensive, that must have been left by mistake. He folded it neatly and put it on the picnic table next to the stack of pamphlets, got out his bag of food and snacks then sat down.

The light wind was rustling through the branches of the forest of trees as he finally settled down from the long troublesome morning and frantic drive up the mountain.

He made a peanut butter and jelly sandwich using one of the pamphlets for a plate and sighed as he took a bite.

All was quiet and peaceful both around and inside of him. He thought about the hippy convention and smiled at the image of the crusty old man romping around with a bunch of young hippy women.

"That must have been quite a scene."

There was a half-burnt book next to the pile of

pamphlets, and the hand-drawn title on the cover said: JEN'S DIARY in big bold letters with happy faced yellow flowers dancing around the title. The pages on the bottom right corner were singed black, it looked like it'd been thrown into a fire and hastily retrieved before it could be burnt into a pile of ashes.

Intrigued, Bob carefully opened the book to the first page with his little finger while munching on the sandwich.

Day 1:

'OMG, this place is amazing, everyone is so carefree and spirited, I LOVE IT, LOVE IT, LOVE IT !!! I'm going to weave flowers in my hair and go to every rainbow sparkling life changing event that I can! This is going to be the best weekend ever !!!'

Day 2:

'It's getting kind of smelly around here. Doesn't anyone ever take a bath ???!!! Some of the classes are fun, but there's a weird vibe in the air, like some weirdo is always staring at me. Maybe it's just me… Like my yoga instructor tells us, we have to let our ego fly away like a little white bird in the sky. Just fly away. I'll try, I'll try…'

Day 3:

'So there I am standing in line, waiting to get into the big tent for the afternoon's Kundalini Yoga Class. I've always wanted to try this class ! It's hot and smelly and

there's a big hairy naked guy standing in front of me and I think a lot of the smells in this whole place are coming from him !!! I'm holding my nose but it's no use. I don't want to lose my place in line, I might not get in ! His back and the rest of his naked dirty body is covered in hair and I think I'm going to puke. I try to let my ego fly away like a little white bird and ignore him, fly away little bird, fly away! And then he bends over to pick up something on the ground IN FRONT OF HIM AND I CANNOT UNSEE THE SIGHT !!!!! GET ME OUT OF HERE !!!! GET ME OUT !!!!'

After the last exclamation point, the pen must have ripped through the paper, and the book thrown into the nearest fire pit, since that was the last entry.

Bob shrugged and pushed the book away from the pile of papers, took another bite of the sandwich and pulled a pamphlet off the top: 'How to survive in a materialistic society.' Sort of boring after reading Jen's Diary.

And the next one: 'Yoga 101, finding your inner circle of strength'. Lame.

And the next one: 'Star meditation.' There was a picture of a man and a woman sitting close together on a mountain looking towards the star filled sky with one large and radiating star above the heads, and the caption at the bottom read: '*Be at one with the Universe*'.

Interesting. He opened it up and read the contents.

Combining the ancient Vipassana breathing meditation techniques with a new age star filled energy attraction you will find your place in eternity.

1. Find a place of solitude far away from city lights, preferably on the top of a high mountain.
2. Close your eyes and focus only on your breathing.
3. Clear your mind of all negativity, sweep them out with an imaginary broom, then use the broom to sweep out all personal thoughts of yourself and the world around you, then use the broom to sweep out all thought completely until your mind is an empty room, free from yourself and your ego.
4. Find a star in the sky and fill your mind with love from the middle of your heart for that star, and with your mind free from your ego, clean and clear and full of love and only love, focus on that one star, and only that star. Funnel all your hopes and dreams and life on that star and be at one with it.

"Wow," he muttered, shaking his head and closing the pages. "That's pretty whacked out." He put the pamphlet down and finished chewing his sandwich in silence.

"Be at one with the universe. I'd like to be at one with my comfy bed back home right now."

It had been one long crazy day, from the phone call in his office to start things off, and now here he was, high in the Sierra mountains with a wood picnic table for a bed.

His eyes became drowsy and he put a stack of pamphlets under his head for a pillow then laid down on the long bench, folded his hands on his chest, dead tired from his journey, and with one long deep breath fell fast asleep.

6.

When he woke up the sun had set long ago, and the park was pitch black. Crickets were chirping in the woods. He opened his eyes and saw the stars straight above twinkling beyond the towering pines. He stretched and yawned, sat up and looked at his watch. Four-thirty.

"You have to be kidding me," he said aloud. "I slept for eight hours on a hard bench and I can't recall having a single dream. I can't even remember being asleep." How he managed to stay on the narrow bench, dead to the world, without rolling onto the hard ground was a mystery.

He was hungry so got the flashlight out of the car and made another peanut butter and jelly sandwich, wolfing it down with a few swigs of juice.

"I wonder if I can get back to sleep?"

He laid back down on the bench and closed his eyes. He tried to hold them shut, squeezing them tight.

Not a chance.

He sat back up again. *So now what?*

I better check my phone, he thought, *what if Sara cooled off and had second thoughts? Here I am on the type of adventure she liked to go on. Maybe she misses me. Maybe I could call her.*

But then he thought better of it as he replayed in his mind her voice over the phone just a few hours ago. She dumped him. Why continue be a loser, and a groveler? *It's no use, she's gone.*

But then again…

He cursed at himself. "Dammit Bob, why can't you just let anything go?"

Grumbling, he flicked on the screen of the phone just in case she might have called. It was empty, no bars, no service. He felt a pang of panic.

What if she did call me? She might have, he thought, stranger things have happened. Maybe she tried to call and left him a message. What if she thought twice about the break-up, called him back to apologize and wanted to get back together and he only had a short time frame to reply?

"No cell phone service, what the hell kind of a campground is this? I need elevation, need to get to higher ground."

The air was so crisp and clear, and the stars so bright that he could see the faint shape of a mound, a hill through a clearing in the trees nearby. It didn't look like it was too far away—and he had a flashlight. His mind made up, he started walking, though immediately stubbed his big toe on a rock and fell to the ground with a yelp.

He held the front of his toe tight with both hands, afraid he would look down and see it split in two or the toenail gone.

After a short while the throbbing eased, and he opened two fingers to get a glimpse. He sighed in relief, the skin was still intact.

"Better wear shoes ya damn hippy," he told himself.

He got his socks and shoes out of the car and slid them on, tied them tight and set off again. Using the flashlight to brighten his path, he walked through the trees, around rocks and boulders and up the hill that rose above the treetops, finally arriving about a hundred feet above the campsite.

He checked his phone again. Still no bars. To his right and hidden from sight by the trees when he was at ground level, was a bigger hill. This one looked like a mini-mountain, towering above nearly three hundred feet in height.

"Let's go," he told himself and started climbing, scaling in some places with the flashlight in his teeth, the angle of ascent growing steeper towards the top. He muscled his way up with fingertips wedged into crevices and toes pushed into the side of the granite hillside. Straining on his belly, he slid over the edge until he finally stood at the top, covered in sweat and dirt, huffing and puffing for air.

Now the campsite was far below him, he was over

three hundred feet above it and he could see over all the treetops to the road he came in on. He was surrounded by towering mountains many thousands of feet higher, but this should be high enough, he thought, unless the entire Sierra Nevada range is blocking my signal. He sat down on the flat-topped peak and opened his phone. Five bars. He held his breath and checked his messages.

He had one message, from some phone number in the city. Still holding his breath, he pressed the play button. It was his landlord with a shrill voice screaming into his phone.

"Bob I'll give you one more day to come up with the rent money, and if you don't hand over every last penny, I'll take all your furniture and sell on auction!"

An old couch, a TV and a bed. His clothes, what were left after his ex-wife threw them in the dumpster, were stuffed into cardboard boxes in the closet.

"You can have it all pal," he whispered as he deleted the message and double checked to see if there were any more.

The message bar read: 0

She hadn't tried to call after all.

To grovel, or not to grovel, that was the question. He tried to convince himself that a simple phone call wasn't actually groveling, it was the polite thing to do. Just checking in on someone who meant a lot to you was both right and proper.

"I'm at the top of a mountain in the middle of the Sierra Nevada in the middle of the night. I've got nothing to lose."

He steeled his nerves by clenching his fist and holding in a breath, then dialed Sara's phone number. Blocked. He tried again. Blocked again. He unclenched his fist while letting out his breath, his self-worth shattered for the last time.

"I've got nothing to lose because I'm a loser."

He wanted to throw the phone far down into the valley below but thought better of it and put it back in his pocket. He closed his eyes and rubbed his forehead before opening them again and taking stock of his situation. He looked over the ledge he was sitting on, down the steep mountain, and he whistled. It's a whole easier going up than down, he thought, so I might as well just stay here till dawn rather than break my neck tumbling down in the dark.

They'd probably never find me if I did fall. The wolves and buzzards would carry me off, bit by bit, and bite by bite.

The stars blazed overhead, and he slowed his thoughts down and marveled at them.

There were a few he recognized from his young days as a Boy Scout and as a Junior Astronomer in High School. It was the middle of summer and the milky way was stretched overhead from north to south. There, setting on the south west horizon was the constellation Scorpio, filling a quarter of the sky, with Antares the red giant star that would someday go supernova anchoring the tail.

And there, rising in the east was the dusty cluster

of stars that looked like a little dipper; Pleiades, followed down and to the right by the V-shaped Taurus and then the three bright stars of Orion's belt that were just clearing the horizon. To the left and above the three stars of the belt was a rusty orange star burning bright and steady, Betelgeuse. It was another red giant that would someday soon also go supernova, some estimates were that it would explode within the next thousand years, which was like a split second in time on the celestial level.

With a diameter a billion miles wide, nearly a thousand times larger than the Sun, Betelgeuse was so large that the Sun would look like a puny little planet next to it, a peanut next to an elephant, and if you placed the center of Betelgeuse right over the Sun, the circumference would extend well past Mars and the asteroid belt and possibly as far as Jupiter nearly five hundred million miles away.

Yet even as giant as it was, at six hundred and forty two light years away, it was still just a small, bright, reddish-colored star.

A light wind rustled through his hair. The sweat from the hike had dried, the anxiety about his ex-girlfriend long since disappeared, and he was breathing in a very slow and easy cadence. It was two in the morning on the top of a mountain and he smiled. Everything was going to be okay. Then he remembered the pamphlet back at the camp; *Star Meditation*.

Be at one with the universe.

"I'll give it a try."

He closed his eyes and imagined a broom in his brain sweeping out negative vibes. It was like cleaning an old house, dust and dirt and cobwebs going right out the door, and he opened his mouth to let the debris fly out. Then he swept out his thoughts of the world, his ego, his name, his history, his entire being, swept it right out the door of his mouth with a long slow exhale, the air of his breath carrying with it like a river carries all the debris and flotsam and jetsam after a rainstorm washes the world clean. Then he forgot what he was supposed to do next.

"Oh yeah," he said out loud with a smile as he remembered. "Pick out a star and fill your heart with love and funnel everything towards that star."

When he opened his eyes he was looking directly at the constellation Orion, the hunter standing tall and ready for battle with Taurus the bull that was towering over him. The hunter with the three bright stars of his belt, the sword hanging down to the left, the shield held high to the right, and to the left a club ready to batter the bull. His shoulder below the club was the bright red star Betelgeuse. The three stars of his belt lined up perfectly equidistant from each other and being the most predominant feature of the constellation he pondered the question.

Which one?

Three of them all lined up, bright and blue and strong, and yet the one on the left was burning brighter, bluer, stronger and he nodded his head in agreement with it.

Yes, you're the one.

Then he remembered the events of the morning, the punch in his gut, the humiliation, and he shook his head. I'm still a loser, and not worthy of a big bright blue star.

What about Betelgeuse? It's a giant red star, an angry super giant that was ready to go supernova any minute. *Kind of like you, right Bob?* he asked himself. Ready to blow up at a moment's notice. Just go ballistic when the next boss or future ex-girlfriend says the wrong thing.

He let that thought wash over him and took a deep breath.

"Just let it go", he whispered and he was humble and meek again.

Let it go. He reached down, picked up a bit of dirt in between his thumb and forefinger, and rubbed them together, grinding the dirt into dust that fell off his fingers into a little pile.

Someday that'll be you Bob, just a pile of dust, so you better be nice.

He raised his eyes to the heavens again.

"I'll have to pick a smaller meeker star, one that matches me."

There above the line of Orion's belt, just a little bit above the red star of Betelgeuse he saw a small tender star with a steady light. It was so close to the super giant red star that he couldn't tell if it was actually a separate star, or just a reflection from Betelgeuse.

It was barely visible, and he squinted his eyes together, then made a little pinhole with the tips of the thumb and forefinger of both hands pressed together. Like a mini telescope blocking everything else around it. It was a tiny star next to the red giant.

"I'll pick you, little star", he thought.

He calmed his breathing, and his pulse rate slowed.

He imagined all his heart and soul funneling out to the star, his two eyes fixed on it, boring into it non-blinking, non-thinking, and he became entranced. His mind went blank and all that remained was his vision, though it was separate from and removed from him; a movie screen in an endless void. A warm feeling permeated his being, and he felt a strange thought, it was a word, and yet it wasn't a word. But it felt like a word that had volume that he could push against and would push back gently, like a large rubber ball that was pressing against his forehead squishy and warm. The word and the ball and the warm feeling all felt/said *friend*, not over and over like a word would be pronounced then followed by silence, but it was a long drawn out continual thought/feeling/vibration of that single word: friend.

"Friend," he whispered, putting into words the feeling that surrounded him. He felt the word leave his body in the substance of resonating sound and breath, he felt as though he were falling, as in a dream when one falls off a cliff, the sudden terror that shakes you awake. A self-preservation caveman-like fear jolted through his body, he felt his ego return suddenly, his heart-rate jumped through the roof, he snapped out of his trance and jumped to his feet scared for his life, ready to run if he had to.

One thing was certain, he wasn't alone.

Someone was invading his space. Paranoid, panicked, with wild darting eyes he searched with a hunter instinct all around the mountain peak where he stood.

Someone else was there.

Crouching, ready to attack, or be attacked, eyes wide, fists clenched, teeth gritted, nostrils flared, a strange animal-like adrenal prickling every hair, making them stand on end.

Attack or be attacked.

He reached down and picked up a rock with one hand and a stick with the other, ready to fight back.

To kill or be killed.

A strange guttural sound, a visceral growl came out of his throat.

Then as quickly as it began, he remembered to breathe, and the feeling of fear passed. The only sound remaining was the pounding of his heart, and that also eased until all he heard was the wind.

He stood there in silence, breathing slow and quiet, knowing that he was truly all alone on the top of the mountain.

"What the hell just happened?" he whispered out loud, scared and confused, yet at the same time completely relieved.

The wind blew softly through the tree tops and

past his ears, and his heart settled into a steady cadence, beating slow and methodical again. He sat down with a heavy sigh and thought hard.

"Maybe I got some sort of weird contact high from the hippies? I ate the sandwiches that I brought with me, and used one of the pamphlets that I found on the table as a plate, maybe there was something on the paper? Some sort of psychedelic drug residue. LSD? Mushroom spores? Maybe that was it. They were using magic mushrooms on the very table that I was eating and sleeping on, and the psilocybin spores were everywhere, I was eating them, breathing them, permeating my skin. I even slept with some of the pamphlets as a pillow, and yet I had no dreams. Something could have seeped through my skull and into my brain. Maybe I've been drugged."

He thoughts plunged deeper then, scrunching his forehead as he went through a list of past events in his life, from childhood through school and work, key events of his entire life, and the events of today. and all were in methodical order. He was a scientist of sorts, in his mind he was a mathematician and a statistician of the highest order.

He ran some mathematical calculations in his brain.

"Two plus five equals seven, ten minus one equals nine."

Quick simple additions and subtractions to begin with, then divisions and multiplications, fractions, algebra, calculus, geometry.

"Five to the fifth power is… three thousand one hundred and twenty five. The area of a circle with a radius of thirteen is….." his mind clicking off the numbers like a calculator. "…Five hundred thirty point nine three."

He was purely analytical, performing a self-assessment on his mental and physical condition.

He stood up, shoulders and back straight, arms shoulder height straight out to the sides, and with his eyes straight ahead, touched each finger and thumb, one after the other to his nose, then to his chin and the middle of his forehead. He reached down and touched each toe of his shoe in succession and then his heels, then stood back up and reached both hands behind his back and touched his fingers together without missing a single connection.

He held his hands straight out at shoulder width, rotated his head and his eyes towards one hand, then to the other and back again, focusing and un-focusing his vision, until he was satisfied that he was in full control of his faculties.

I am not drugged, he concluded. *It was probably some sort of strange anomaly that I experienced.*

I've been through a combination of physical and spiritual abuse, he reminded himself. *I'm tired, sad, beaten down and emotionally vulnerable, while at the same time I feel somewhat elated, being here on top of this mountain surrounded by stars. I'm also at a higher elevation than I was this morning, it was a struggle getting up here and the oxygen content is smaller due to the corresponding lighter air pressure.*

A tiny thought crept into the back of his mind. What if the pamphlet instructions were the true key? What if they actually worked and he had in fact suddenly become one with the universe?

He scoffed and laughed out loud at the thought, then laughed again for good measure, his sense of humor had returned.

"Why that's the first time I've laughed today," he said.

He sat down again and looked at the stars with a new attitude, with a happy heart. Everything was going to be okay.

What the heck, he thought, *I'll try again, what harm can it do? It's all in good fun.*

"Be at one with the Universe," he whispered.

He slowly shut his eyes, like two butterflies closing their wings together, concentrated on his breathing and nothing else. Then got out the broom and opened his mouth to sweep out the bad thoughts, along with all his ego, and this time when he opened his eyes again, he knew exactly what to do. He funneled all the warmth in his heart towards the tiny little star in the constellation Orion.

His breathing slowed to nothing while the star filled his entire being, taking the place of his other self and he heard/felt/thought the word again: friend, a long drawn out single word. He whispered back, "friend", with his lips and his inner being, and he said it again in a long drawn out way: "friend." He realized that he wasn't alone, but this time he was ready and not afraid. Someone else was with him, not with him here, but inside whatever it was that was carrying that word with it. Whatever it was like a warm, soft rubber ball pressed against the top of his forehead. Suddenly, he was floating.

The little star in Orion blurred, his spirit being consciousness stretched like taffy flowing out of his body, and he travelled out and above himself until the earth disappeared in the blink of an eye, and he was on a different, higher mountain, the edge of the sky by the horizon a reddish orange haze. High above that horizon the sky was clear and black, filled with a different and strange arrangement of stars and constellations. A fantastic nebula filled half the sky and the world down below was dark and covered with a maze of roads and houses, round and small and set apart in perfect order. Lights bordered a long, straight highway that lead to a gigantic city of tall skyscrapers, dimly lit on the edges.

For a moment Bob was afraid. Even though it was strangely similar, he knew without a doubt that this was not Earth.

It was like one of those out-of-body experiences that people described when they died and came back to life, when they were dead and floating above their corpse looking down at it, only in this case he wasn't looking back at his body, he was for all essence *in* another body, in a strange world.

He was standing on the edge of a plateau at the top

of a steep mountain. Spread out on the flat plains below were grids of lights that led, in rows, towards towering skyscrapers in the distance.

The sky above was dark yet filled with pinpoints of stars. It was not as bright as on Earth, since half the sky on the entire right-hand side was filled with a multi colored luminescent cloud. It was not moving but it looked like it was expanding towards the city and would engulf it within moments.

"What is that thing in the sky?" he wondered aloud.

His gaze rotated until the object was centered in his vision, the image filled the entire frame of his sight. He was silent as he studied the magnificence of it.

This was the stuff that the universe was made from. A nebula could be a star being born, heavy gasses swirling together until their gravity brought them together into a star. They could also be created by stars collapsing upon themselves and exploding into a supernova.

Supernovas created nebulas. Is that what this was?

The unmoving cloud of gas, sharp irregular edges, was iridescent with alternating colors of orange, red, green, and bright white. It was in the shape of an oblong sphere, not perfectly round, but like a smoke ring of radiation debris blown out from a cigar-puffing giant on the other side of the universe.

Bob had seen nebula in large telescopes, but these were on the other side of the milky way galaxy, hundreds and thousands of light years away. The crab nebula was over six thousand light years away and even on the clearest nights was just a faint tiny smudge with a pair of binoculars.

The nebula in Orion, in the middle of the sword of the hunter, just below the three stars of the hunter's belt, was nearly twelve hundred light years away. That nebula had a long, leading edge with the trailing cloud diffused and dimming far behind it.

The structure of this one hovering over the strange city was nearly round in shape and appeared to be so close Bob thought he could almost hear the irradiated debris from the explosion approaching, sizzling through the vacuum of space.

It was frightening.

What is it? he wondered again.

The thought pronouncement that came into his mind, rolling like distant drums was matter of fact, and definitive.

Death.

He was silent again as he pondered the significance of that statement. There was no escaping it. He felt his blood pressure rise.

His eyes remained on it for another moment then his vision rotated to the wide plateau around him. He was surrounded by a vast sea of faces that were all looking directly at him.

Thousands upon thousands of upturned faces lightly illuminated by the starlight and the nebula.

How can they see me? he thought. *How do they*

know I'm here?

A sea of eyes watching him.

Who are they and why are they looking at me? Bob was becoming more frightened, and he heard/felt a gentle wash of music-filled words flow through him.

They are all friends.

The faces were hopeful, gentle. All with long dark hair and shining black eyes, nebula and starlight glinting off their corneas.

Where am I? he wondered.

There was a long-measured answer, not words that he was physically hearing with his ears, but more like a song or a melody in his mind that translated into a simple language that he could somehow fully and completely understand.

With me.

The sound of her voice flowed through him, filling his awareness with a golden glow.

A loving compassionate feeling of the presence of another caring being was reassuring and comforting.

Who are you?" he asked.

When the reply came, it was as though an orchestra was playing in a cathedral with the music resonating off the walls and throughout the tall arches, echoing down through his skin to the bones. The bones themselves seemed as if they were tuned to the harmonics of the notes.

Reeevvvaaaa.

The sound of her name moved like smooth stones at the edge of the ocean being rolled around in the shore break. His bones were those stones at the edge of the water, and they rattled with the sound.

Reeevvvaaaaa.

Her name was Reva, and he knew she was a woman, since in his mind Bob felt the presence of a female, a vision of a goddess, dressed in silk with golden skin and long dark flowing hair.

How is this possible?

Even though he wasn't in his body, he was filled with a feeling of some type of inner warmth. A sliver of a memory flashed on the outskirts of his awareness and he grasped at it, but it was elusive.

The sensation was pure, simple, and could not be put into words.

I've felt this way before, he thought.

Then the memories of his past came rushing back. When he was young, when he was in kindergarten or first grade, a pretty little girl in his class sat nearby him.

Long hair, bright eyes, glowing cheeks above a lively shining smile. A faint woozy sensation hollowed out a pit in the center of his stomach. His heart was both sinking and elated while a mixture of infinite hope and impending doom swirled about him.

Puppy love.

Of course, this was the exact same feeling.

Without seeing the other being that he was with, he felt as if he were one with her. He felt her breathing, air rushing into and out of lungs, and as he did so he knew that she could also feel his breathing.

There was a question being posed with a simple thought.

What are you breathing? he wondered.

Four unmistakable images came into his mind.

The first and largest was a nitrogen molecule:

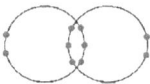

The second, a quarter the size of the previous image, was an oxygen molecule:

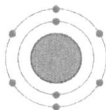

The third, the argon molecule, was one eightieth the size of the first:

The fourth was a tiny microscopic carbon dioxide molecule:

Now, creeping into the forefront of his mind was a hopeful invitation for Bob to show what he was breathing.

He could feel the anxiety in the question that was suddenly clear and concise: *What are you breathing?*

He was first and foremost a statistician, and yet one of his little side hobbies was knowing all types of trivia, facts and figures, including the chemistry of the air that he breathed every day.

He remembered with clarity the first day he decided to know everything he could about the world around him. Long ago in grade school the question was posed to the entire classroom about knowing what it was that they ate, how important it was to know what they were putting into their bodies. That's when he decided to find out what it was they were all breathing. Why not know what it is that you draw into your lungs all day long?

The average person takes sixteen breaths a minute, nine hundred sixty per hour, twenty-three thousand a day, eight and a half million per year. That's a lot of breathing. It seemed to Bob at a very young age that it would be nice to know what was in the air that your life depended on every minute of every day.

He envisioned the numbers in his mind and Reva saw them with him.

This is what I breathe at sea level on the surface of my world, he thought, focusing on his answer.

Nitrogen 78.084%.

Oxygen 20.946%

Argon 0.9340%

Carbon Dioxide 0.04%

He focused on each molecule in turn, from the largest percentage to the lowest. The numbers were definitive and there was not a single doubt in his mind that they were correct.

There was a shift in the combined mood of their minds. From anxiety to quiet relief.

Then a thought was floated to Bob as though it was a whisper drifting down from the wind in the trees.

Help us. It was a soft plea yet edged with a feeling of fear and imminent doom.

His vision rotated to the thousands of faces staring up at him, then back again to the nebula. It appeared to be growing larger.

What can I possibly do? thought Bob.

If you give me permission, I will visit you.

And that is when a sudden wedge of doubt in Bob's mind separated them.

From Orion? How? Skepticism rose into the forefront of his thoughts. *Impossible.*

She insisted. Fear of loss permeated her thought. He could feel it.

Hold out your hands, her anxious voice said in his head. *And keep your mind open and free. I will attempt a great leap. I will visit you to see if I can survive on your planet for a single split second or a day. I will sacrifice my life to save my people. But you must give me permission.*

Bob's vision was centered on the nebula. He was frozen in fear by it.

Help us.

It was a request and yet also a command.

You must hold your hands out, she continued. *I must come directly to your outstretched hands.*

Then she repeated the conditions. *You have to give me complete and total permission to come to you. It is the only way.*

Bob sighed in disbelief, the air in his lungs leaving in a long-controlled stream, that simple act making him lose total contact with Reva. His eyes opened to slits, and he was suddenly conscious of his surroundings back on top of the little hill on Earth, the wind rustling through the tall pines above his head, wisping his hair around and tickling the edges of his ears. The crisp mountain air tinged with the musky smell of earthen rock and soil mixed with pine sap all around him.

This was real, his eyes and his ears and his nostrils told him that the world upon which he was alive, and breathing was on the top of a hill near Lake Tahoe, not some strange faraway world in the constellation Orion.

This is here, this is now, this is all there is, he thought, trying to comfort himself. *This is all there ever was and ever will be. Whatever I just saw was just a dream, nothing more than an illusion.*

And yet his heart told him different. He felt the sound of a name drawing him.

Water at the edge of the ocean rolling round stones together, reverberating through his bones.

Reva.

He was suddenly lonely without his new-found friend. Whether or not he was dreaming was irrelevant at this point and time in his life.

For a few short minutes he'd felt something simple, untainted and pure, and he wanted it back.

His indecisiveness was slowly replaced by a complete and un-moving resolve.

"What have I got to lose?" he whispered to the wind in the trees. Then he focused his eyes on the tiny little star next to Betelgeuse, his breathing slowed, and he kept his mind open and free and full of the thought of Reva.

Friend, she whispered to him across the depth of space.

"Friend," he whispered back and tried to will his way back across the long stretch of space.

He could feel her thoughts intertwining with his. His thoughts that were once haphazard and selfish turned magnanimous and secure.

He held out his hands and waited while a strange trance overwhelmed him, and he lost all sense of self.

Floating, his mind torn into two places at the same time, his spirit looked at itself in the mirror and shined back at him.

Time stood still across the chasm of the universe, in the space where he was and the space where she was, melded into one. He could sense it like a gel that held together everything that existed at that instant of time all across the span of existence, surpassing time and light itself. It was like a gel holding the universe in place, every moment the same across the whole...

There was a loud POP like a dull firecracker suddenly exploded next to him, as the human-sized pocket of air was suddenly displaced by a solid body.

Bob jerked involuntarily at the sound and opened

his eyes, now completely in the here and now on his little mountaintop on the planet Earth.

He wasn't alone.

She lay face-up with her eyes closed, gently holding his hands. A slight red phosphorescent glow and a white mist surrounded her naked body, rising a few inches from her skin then slowly fading away.

Bob couldn't breathe, his chest felt tight, his heart was racing, his blood pressure going through the roof, he could hear the pounding of his heart in the blood veins in his ears as he looked down at her then gently let go of her hands and laid her arms across her chest as he felt himself slowly losing consciousness.

Blackness crept over him.

He passed out quickly. From his sitting position, collapsing into a crumpled heap next to her.

7.

It could have been seconds, or hours before he finally woke up again, slowly regaining consciousness from a dream, or an all-night bender with a bottle of booze.

His head hurt, throbbing from the inside out as though he'd been drinking all night with no food and was horribly hungover. His ears were ringing, his tongue was dry, and his stomach turned into knots. Skin parched on his forearms and moist, clammy on the back of his neck. He felt hungover, and yet somehow not.

His pillow was a pile of tiny rocks, one of them poking into the back of his head, his left hand laying across his chest, while his right hand was in the dirt next to his hip. He spread the fingers of his right hand apart, then brought them together with a handful of dust, rubbing the mixture between his fingers and thumb and the inside of the palm, regaining the feeling in his extremities.

This is what it's like to wake up after getting your lights punched out or having a rock fall on your head. He tried to blink his eyes into focus. He was on his back looking straight up at the fuzzy star-filled sky framed by hundred-foot-tall pine trees. His vision still seemed blurred, so he continued blinking until his eyesight finally focused and the stars became crisp white pinpoint lights piercing down at him through the night. He must have fallen on his head and had a bad dream.

To his right he could see the light of the impending dawn illuminating the forest around him in a colorless and shadowless scene.

Then he remembered.

Reva.

He turned his head slowly to the left and saw the outline of a woman next to him, her strange perfumed scent in his nostrils. He gathered himself into a sitting position and looked down at her nude body.

"She's human," he whispered. "But not…"

No human woman could possibly be this exotic and beautiful.

Even in the colorless light of the approaching dawn, he could see that her skin was a rusty reddish brown, smooth and thick. Hair long, shiny, black and straight, spread out on the ground past her waist, with thick strands covering her breasts down to her knees, her hands, fingers, arms, legs, feet, and even toes…

"You are human," he whispered again. But the doubt remained.

She stirred, her chest moving ever so slightly, small breaths going in and out through her mouth and nose.

"Namalamanse," she whispered out loud. And then simultaneously in his mind he felt the word rolling through him: *friend*.

Bob laid the silk dress over her and her eyelids fluttered open, eyeballs black as coal, gentle, kind, sparkling, looking up at him.

"Friend," Bob whispered towards her.

She could hear/see/feel the word in her/their mind and see how his mouth shaped the word. She repeated it in a soft voice, the air gently leaving her lips, "Friend."

Then, she spoke in her language to him and he heard the physical words whispered from her lips. "Xlandimaka bashi quor gethema petti." While at the same time in his mind he heard the words, *Thank you for inviting me.*

His throat was dry and he gulped before replying: "Oh, it was nothing."

Time stood still as they watched each other, their eyes connected in a silent attraction.

He was entranced by her eyes. *They're black like onyx*, he thought.

She was also spellbound by his eyes and looked at them with amazement, she had never seen anything like them.

Blue like the sky, was the thought that drifted from her mind to his.

He slowly reached out his hand, afraid of what he might find. She put her palm on top of his then brought his hand towards her face, placing it on the side. He felt the firm softness of her cheek, ran his fingers lightly up towards her eyebrows, then up farther across her forehead where her long hair began, pushed the locks away from and revealing her ear, then followed the top of it with light fingers down along the bottom edge of the curved lobe, lingering for a moment, then down along her neckline to her shoulder, rolling the palm of his hand over the rounded edge, then back again over the bony protrusion at the top of the collarbone, continuing down along her triceps to the forearm and back to her hand, curling each finger one at a time, then the thumb, then with the tip of his forefinger lightly circled the soft tissue at the center of her palm. She giggled softly as the skin was tickled then pulled back her hand.

You're real, yes or no? he thought the question with his mind as a test.

Yes, she said back to him with her mind.

"You can hear my voice in your mind and also in your ears, yes?" he asked out loud.

She remained motionless, then floated the thought to him without moving her lips.

Yes.

Then she took a long slow breath, her nostrils flaring on the edges as she smelled the air, and an overwhelming feeling of joy swept over her. A luxurious sigh resonated from her throat through her lips.

I am still alive, she thought to him, round black eyes boring through him.

"Yes," he answered both in thought and word.

She was watching him as he answered, carefully observing the shape of his mouth and the volume of air as it passed his lips.

"Yes," she whispered back.

This is irrational, he thought. *How can this be happening*? Then out loud: "I'm going crazy. No?"

"No," she whispered.

"Did you just say 'no' because you were repeating after me?"

She thought for a moment and then answered again with her voice.

"No."

Fear rose in the back of his mind, his breathing stopped, and his eyes widened. What for a moment seemed completely normal, took on the surreal. His head felt faint again as he watched her.

She reached her hand out and touched his right hand again, then with both hands held his hand till his breathing steadied.

She slowly sat up and looked around at the world, the trees rustling in the wind, the rock that she sat upon, and then up at the stars. She was searching for the place where she came from, the sky was strange. He pointed to the east.

"Orion's belt. Three stars aligned, and above and

to the left is a bright red star. The star I concentrated on is a tiny white star right next to the red star. You see it?"

"Yes."

Bob's eyes followed hers. She saw it alright, she was looking directly at the red flickering star that signaled her world and her entire race's demise.

Her blood pressure went up a notch, and his followed.

"That's Betelgeuse," he said.

Death star, was the thought swirling about in her mind, and she looked back at him, coal black eyes resigned with dread and a slow burning fear.

"Death star," he said out loud. She watched the shape of his lips as the air exited his mouth but did not repeat the words.

In his mind he still saw the nebula hurtling towards her planet through the emptiness of space.

So, it was Betelgeuse, the red supergiant in the constellation Orion that had somehow already gone supernova and was an event that had not yet been seen on Earth.

"Kamanalea onakapa koanella," she said out loud, while in Bob's mind he heard the words. "*Please help us.*"

He tried to repeat the words, but it was no use.

"I'm a mathematician, not a linguist," he said. "I failed Spanish in high school."

One of his favorite books growing up as a child was *Robinson Crusoe,* a story about a man marooned on a desert island, heartbroken and alone, who makes friends with a native and teaches him his language.

"I think it will be better if I teach you to talk in my language," he said. "After all, you're on my planet now. Yes?"

She watched his lips, then answered out loud. "Yes."

"You understand, don't you? You can hear my thoughts in your language, while at the same time hear them with your ears in my language. That's why you didn't just repeat everything that I said but answered with one word in the affirmative. You understand me?"

"Yes," she said again.

"In this case you can also add 'I understand' to the sentence."

It was another test.

"Yes, I understand," she said simply.

It was a start.

8.

Through the rest of the early morning hours he spoke to her as she watched his lips, repeating some of the words and phrases when he paused. He told her all about his life and all about the world that he lived in, from the beginning to now, from his childhood through school and work in the city to his trek up the mountain. It didn't take too long before he ran out of things to say about himself and his life.

He went through the alphabet, then pulled up a website on his phone and read poems, the first pages of great novels, news stories, weather reports, the world's greatest jokes, then when his voice was getting hoarse and wearing out from talking, as the orange glow from the sunrise lit the edge of the world, they both fell sound asleep.

When the morning sun was well over the horizon, clear and bright, shining through the pine forest and warming the air, Reva gently pushed on Bob's shoulder.

He was sound asleep with a folded evergreen branch under his head as a pillow. He was snoring, suffering through a nightmare.

In his dream, the sun was exploding in a fiery ball of flames, aliens were chasing him down a cold, dark ravine. He couldn't get away, his legs wouldn't move, he looked down at them and urged them to run but they were struck in the sand. Then one of the aliens had him by the shoulder, pulling him backwards into an abyss.

He woke up with a start, snorting air, eyes fluttering then popping wide open to see a concerned Reva looking down at him with her hand on his arm.

Out of the dark chasm of his dream to the reality of the here and now, he suddenly remembered the night and his breathing intensified for a moment. It slowed again as he studied her face, letting the memories rush back to him.

"You're not a dream," he said, "You're real."

"Yes," she answered with her voice. "I'm real."

He sensed an impatience building within her. They'd already gone over this during the night. She was impatient with him, the same as an earth woman would be, and he smiled at her with humor in his eyes.

"Are you sure you're an alien from another planet?"

There a sparkle in her coal black eyes that crinkled at the edges with a bit of mischievousness, her mouth drawing into a smile of her own. She didn't use her voice but only replied by thought.

Maybe you're the alien, and I'm dreaming you.

He could hear her voice clearly in his mind, and his smile quickly faded as his jaw slackened. In a way it was terrifying.

"You called to me and I answered," she said. "I have been searching, we have all been searching, everyone on our planet, for someone, anyone."

"Searching how? By wishing on a star?" Because in a strange way, that is what I was doing."

"We have all been searching the heavens for many years, many generations. You saw them on the plateau outside the city last night. Thousands upon thousands of my people. Each of us assigned to a different star every night for hundreds of years. Finally, out of the millions of stars that we called out to, you Bob have found us. You found me. You saw the nebula. A star nearby has collapsed. You call it Betelgeuse. We call it the death star."

"Over a thousand years ago, my ancestors realized that Betelgeuse would soon explode in a supernova. We could see that the weight of the star was collapsing upon its core, this process had taken many thousands of years, and yet it was suddenly accelerating. Once it got to the critical mass it would explode within a microsecond. We thought we had anywhere from a day to, at most, a thousand years. We missed the long estimate by a few hundred years."

There was a nagging feeling in the back of Bob's mind. "When did it go supernova?"

"Five hundred years ago. We survived the gamma ray burst, but we will not survive the shock wave that is coming."

Bob's mind spun. Betelgeuse was six hundred and forty two lights years away. They wouldn't see the light from the explosion for another hundred and forty odd years from now. He thought back to his astronomy days. At one time he was intrigued with supernovas and black holes. When a star collapsed and imploded it emitted a short burst of gamma and x-rays that traveled nearly the speed of light, invisible and deadly. After that, the protons and electrons that made up most of the mass of the star melted into each other to become a city-sized neutron star with a super compact mass. A star's mass that was once a billion miles wide compressed into an area as wide as New York City. A neutron star was so dense that a single teaspoon of it could weigh as much as ten million tons.

"You survived the gamma burst. How?"

"By tunneling deep in the planet and hiding. The burst was short lived, less than one day, and we were ready. We had been planning for the event for many generations. We built tunneling machines. Deep in the planet we built concrete and steel bunkers to hide throughout the onslaught of x-rays, gamma rays, neutrinos. We knew we could save ourselves, but we couldn't save everything on the planet. Every living creature on the surface of the planet, and everything within a few hundred meters of the surface of the oceans, was destroyed. Half of our ozone layer was also destroyed, and now the ultraviolet radiation from our own sun is a threat to our existence. The ratio of oxygen to the rest of the gasses in our atmosphere plunged with the depletion of green plants and the plankton in the oceans. We built giant cold plasma ozone machines and pumped it into the atmosphere, so we could at least live on the surface of the planet again. It took a long time to get it back to a level where we could live on the surface during the day, but we still had to have special clothing to protect our skin, which darkened over a few generations. Our farms are protected with a special type of shade cloth that blocks ultraviolet radiation."

"How could you know…"

"The exact time of the event? We sent out sentinels in spacecraft straight towards the doomed star. They warned us."

"Gamma rays travel the speed of light. Nothing is faster than the speed of light, so how could they warn you?"

"Thought waves are instantaneous. There is no measurable speed. They just are."

"They gave their lives to warn us. We survived the gamma burst, which gave us a little more time. But the shock wave is coming. We estimated that the shock wave was travelling at about ten percent of the speed of light, and since the supernova was fifty light years from us, we would have around five hundred years, give or take a few years."

"We also built hundreds of self-contained robot-controlled spaceships, cryogenically freezing some of our best and brightest, and launched them towards different stars, hoping to get enough of a head start and distance to outrun the shock wave."

"With a slingshot from the orbit of our sun they have a top speed of sixty-seven thousand miles per hour. At that speed they'd have to travel a thousand hours to get one hour ahead of the shock-wave. Time was not on our side. To get to the nearest star at that rate would take thousands of years, with no guarantee of a planet to land on. We were doomed if the star exploded."

"Once we determined that the shockwave was imminent and there was no escaping, we sent new sentinels in spaceships towards the approaching nebula to be our early warning devices, but this time it would signal the very end. We call them the watchers. The farthest one from our planet was sent over twenty-five years ago, and that watcher was nearing the end of his days."

Was nearing the end. Past tense.

"Show me," he said.

Reva held out her hands again and he grabbed them lightly.

They were looking out of a portal on a small space ship. The window was round and curved on the outside into the shape of a lens, a telescope of sorts and in the middle of the lens. Nearly filling the entire portal was a bright red ball of flame, seething, flickering on the edges.

It was the same nebula from Betelgeuse that he'd seen on Reva's planet. Only this one occupied the entire sky from end to end.

It expanded, growing until it filled the portal, then the vision ended in blackness. They both felt a sort of jolt at the end, which was the end of the watcher.

"This just happened?" he asked.

"Five days ago. The shock wave is coming. Travelling at sixty-seven million miles per hour it will scorch the atmosphere off the surface of our planet, knock it off its axis and out of orbit. Every plant and creature will be incinerated in the blink of an eye. Every mountain will be leveled, every valley will be filled. And there is nothing we can do to stop it.'

Bob bit his lower lip as he looked at her. A couple of hours ago, he wouldn't have thought it possible to transport a peanut even an inch, yet alone a living, breathing being across the vast extent of space. But now...

"What do you want from me?"

"I will stay with you Bob. If I can survive two days here on your planet, I'll ask you for permission to transport more of my people here."

Ask permission to bring an alien population to Earth.

"Why do you need permission, why don't you just do it, and bring them over right now?"

She shook her head. "We could never do that. Our civilization, our lives are based on cooperation and agreement on everything that we do."

"Okay, you need our help, and I'm not sure the best way to go about this. We could go to the authorities and ask for their help, ask for assistance, but that may take too much time, and they might put me in the loony bin. We have an old saying: 'sometimes it's easier to ask for forgiveness than permission.'"

She stood up and stretched her arms over her head, breathing deep while leaning backwards, lean and strong limbs uncoiling.

Bob was entranced. He'd never in all his days seen a beauty such as her. Black-as-night hair cascading down her sides and flowing past her knees.

She walked over to the side of mountain, looked over the rubble strewn terrain, then bent over and picked up a round rock the size of a loaf of bread. She placed it on her shoulder, walked to the gnarled base of the bristlecone pine tree, and set it down so that it gently touched the bark.

"What's the rock for?" he asked.

"This is for remembrance, to commemorate this day. This rock has been moved to a new place, as have I. It also reminds me that even though this rock is hard and strong, someday it will be turned to dust, and I, while not nearly as strong, will turn to dust much sooner."

She sat next to it, placing her hand on it while closing her eyes. Bob let her be and stayed quiet while watching her. It was as though she were praying over it. Then after many long moments, she opened her eyes and stood up. Together, they walked down the side of the mountain.

9.

They sat on the picnic table at the campsite next to the blue car. It was cool and shady under the towering pine trees. She sat across from him watching his lips as he read to her from his computer pad.

It was soothing for her to listen to his voice both with her ears and through her mind, slowly understanding the cadence and meaning of the words in the English language. Earlier in the day he read a book called *The Iliad*, then skipped through some of Shakespeare's play *All's Well That Ends Well,* then a few chapters of Hemingway and Steinbeck for good measure. Now he was reading *Fear and Loathing in Las Vegas*, tracing the sentences with his finger on the screen, then waiting for her to repeat them.

She was getting good.

They could hear the crunch of tires on gravel approaching from the north. They watched as an old black truck rolled up around the corner and into the clearing. It was the old man, the owner of the campground. Too late to try and hide her, and what good would it do anyway, she was here.

The only noticeable difference between Reva and a human woman, besides her incredible beauty, were her coal black eyes.

"Here, put these on," said Bob indicating quickly how to wear them, and handed her his sunglasses that were sitting on the table. "Don't worry, everything's okay."

The old man got slowly out of his truck and walked towards them with his cane, smiling wide. Smiling at Reva.

"Well, I hope you had a nice night at our little camp." He was beaming, and stood a little straighter, trying to show off for her. "I didn't know you had a lady friend with you."

"Yes, well she was asleep in the back seat when I arrived last night."

"I hope you slept well ma'am."

It was a question. She recognized that it necessitated an answer.

"Yes," said Reva and gave a Mona Lisa smile without showing him her teeth.

"You know," said the old man. "Around these parts we greet each other with a hug."

Dirty old man, thought Bob and he put up his hand. "Well, we're not from around here." And wasn't that the truth, especially as far as Reva was concerned.

The old man, brushed off the slight and became

more business-like, straightening his thin frame and lifting his chin while looking down his long nose at them. "Well, anyhow I just stopped by to pick up the rest of this trash." He motioned to the stack of pamphlets. "Sorry you had to spend the night with all this rubbish around, ma'am."

The old man looked at Reva, boring his eyes into her, for some reason waiting for an answer to his question. A more thorough answer than just a simple yes or no. Was he testing her? Did he think she might be an illegal from south of the border and want to call the cops in retaliation for a rejected hug. You never could tell with people.

No problem, thought Bob and right on cue Reva repeated in her own voice and in perfect English:

"No problem."

It was a pleasant evening under the stars, thought Bob.

"It was a pleasant evening under the stars," said Reva in perfect pitch and pronunciation, with a stoic face, as she concentrated on repeating precisely what Bob was thinking.

My God I'm like the ultimate ventriloquist, thought Bob. She started to repeat his last thought and he put his finger gently on her lips to quiet her.

The old man squinted his eyes at her, frowned, let out a raspy harrumph from the center of his throat, leaned on his cane then walked back to his truck. He looked down at his watch and turned back towards them again.

"Check-out time is high noon, and it's eleven-thirty. Will you be staying another night?" He asked with a hopeful tone in his voice.

Just thinking about this crusty old guy, with him knowing that Reva was here and possibly lurking around, hiding behind a tree in the woods with binoculars made Bob sick to his stomach. *Not a chance*, thought Bob and was about to merely tell the old man 'no thanks', but Reva answered out loud:

"Not a chance."

The old man looked as though he'd been slapped in the face, and was crushed for a moment, stunned to silence.

It was kind of you to stop by, thought Bob.

"It was kind of you to stop by," said Reva and her heart went out to him.

The beginning of a faint smile appeared on the old man's face then grew and grew until it was stretched from ear to ear and he suddenly looked ten years younger. He'd also been humbled and it showed within the deep wrinkles on his brow and down through his worn cheeks.

"Why thank you ma'am," he said softly, then bowed slightly and tipped his cap to her, lifted his old frame into the truck and drove slowly away.

Reva was looking at Bob with a curious expression. *Why?* she was thinking. Then she said it out loud, free from the constraints of merely thinking the thought.

"Why?"

"Why what?" asked Bob.

"Why did you want me to say: 'it was kind of you to stop by'?"

Bob shrugged his shoulders. "His feelings were hurt when you told him 'not a chance' to his question about us staying another day. I didn't really want you to say that to him, I was merely thinking it and you suddenly said it out loud. When you told him it was kind of him to stop by, it soothed him and made him feel better. We don't want to hurt anyone after all."

She didn't say or think anything in reply to his statement while deep in her own thoughts. Then she said out loud:

"Love all, trust a few, do wrong to none."

"Shakespeare. You have a good memory. That's a line from one of the stories I just read you."

"Who is he?"

"Was. Who was he, since he's long gone," said Bob.

"But how can he be gone if his words still live?"

Bob squinted at her and tilted his head. "Right you are Miss Reva. He was a poet who lived on the other side of the planet about two hundred years ago, and his words do indeed live on as I've just witnessed, spoken at an opportune time by a beautiful alien from another planet. Amazing."

"Amazing," she repeated, rolling it over her tongue and relishing in the sound and feel and meaning. She smiled, and said to him. "I like that word."

Bob smiled back at her and pointed towards his

car. "Let's go for a ride."

She hesitated. He could see it in her eyes, and feel it in her thoughts.

"Do you have vehicles on your planet?"

"Yes."

"Anything like this?"

She shrugged her shoulders. "How is it powered?"

"Internal gasoline combustion engine." He reached through the driver's side window under the console and pulled a lever and the hood clicked open a crack, then he went to the front and undid the safety latch and opened the hood for her to have a look. Subconsciously Bob felt a sense of pride, as though he himself had some hand in the planning, engineering and manufacturing of the car, when all he really did was go down to the lot and pick it out from a hundred other similar models. He could change a tire and fill the radiator, but that was about all.

As she looked under the hood at the jumble of hoses and metal parts, he could sense a frown on her face.

"What do you think?"

"It looks very…" She struggled for a word but he knew what she was thinking so finished the sentence for her.

"…complicated."

"Yes, it looks very complicated. But that's not the word I was looking for. It looks very…" And she struggled again, until he realized the word she was searching for and his sense of pride in the human engineering of the car evaporated.

"Primitive?" he ventured.

"Yes," she smiled. That was the word she was looking for. "It looks very primitive. There are many tubes and wires and it looks like any one of them could malfunction and cause the engine to stop."

Isn't that the truth, he thought as he recalled some of the car problems he'd encountered in the past. Damn all the wires and tubes. He morphed into defensive mode.

"Well, we're working on that."

As though he were personally working on the solution.

"This is an old style of engine," he continued. "That's on its way out. Someday soon every car on the planet will be run on electricity, and those engines are a lot simpler, I can tell you that. We're just working on a few small problems. Like how to store the electricity, for one."

She smiled at him. The thought he felt in his mind was "*poor little humans*", in a polite and humorous way.

10.

They drove out of the campsite and down the dusty road.

Circling first east and then south they skirted the western edge of Lake Tahoe, the emerald blue water showing itself now and then, teasingly through the trees and houses that blocked the full view of the water. Reva leaned over him, and the steering wheel, to get a better look. She was oohing and aahing, small cooing sounds coming out of her throat, and Bob decided it would be safest to pull over somewhere so she could get a better look rather than having her grab the steering wheel and sending them into the oncoming traffic.

Halfway down the lake on the right was a sign that said "Timberland," while on the left was another sign that read "Hurricane Bay." The road edged closer to the lake then ran along the side of it, close enough to throw a bagel out of the window and hit the water. Small piers jutted out from the land and boats large and small dotting the shoreline, moored just off shore.

Bob found a good enough looking private spot and pulled over. He parked under a pine tree with the passenger side window facing the lake.

Reva leaned out the window, breathing long and deep. The fresh air, with a breeze coming across the lake, was chilled and sweet. She looked puzzled for a moment, trapped in the car and longing to find a way out. Bob thought she might crawl out the window at any minute and he reached over and pulled up on the handle. The offending door gave way to a shriek of delight as Reva bounded out and ran to the water's edge.

Barefoot, in men's shorts and t-shirt she walked confidently to the lake and let the tiny waves gently wash over her toes and ankles. She crossed her arms in front of her and lifted her head to the sky, in prayer or thanks, Bob had no clue. He decided to join her, kicked off his sandals and walked across the dark gritty sand and into the cold water next to her. He yelped a little at the nippy temperature and Reva laughed with, and at, him.

I love this, she thought. He heard her in his mind, and he nodded.

"Do you have places like this?" he asked her out loud.

She narrowed her eyes and replied. "Yes, many." Here the lake was about ten miles wide, and her gaze travelled across the water. He followed it to the other side where the mountains rose, and they could both see tall buildings and homes dotting the hillsides.

"We call this a lake," he said.

"We have many lakes on our planet." She looked back at him with mischievousness in the corners of her eyes. "In fact, we have a lake that is almost half the size of the planet."

"Half the size, you say?"

She nodded with a feigned superior look while raising her chin.

It was a playful challenge he couldn't resist.

"We call that an ocean, and we have one too, but ours is over three quarters of our entire planet." He raised his chin to match hers.

She smiled sweetly. *Water means life*, she thought. *Your planet is most blessed*.

Out of the corner of his eyes, Bob saw movement. What was once a perfect empty place to see the lake up close was soon to change.

A young couple was jogging towards them along the edge of the water over a hundred yards away but travelling fast, laughing and joking as they ran, dressed in colorful designer running gear, sleek and tanned, and Bob stepped to the side of Reva to block her as much as he could from their view as they passed, but it was to no avail. He could see the looks in their eyes as they got closer, their outlook turned from smiling happy and carefree to concerned and wary as they passed. The young man edged the woman he was with so that they passed well to the side, in a semi-circle around Bob and Reva. It was strange to see someone go so far out of their way to avoid them.

Bob watched them and smiled and gave a little wave, but they did not wave back and picked up their pace, whispering to each other as they passed.

"Let's go," said Bob and reached out for Reva's hand. She was disappointed, not wanting to leave the water, but she relented and walked next to him back to the car.

When can we go back to the water? she thought hopefully.

"Soon," he replied out loud.

Bob looked over at Reva in a realistic way. She looked normal enough, maybe for Hollywood boulevard at midnight. But not here in Lake Tahoe, or most other places in the world for that matter. With her coal black eyes, long wild dark hair, reddish tanned skin and sharp features while wearing men's clothes she looked like a female punk rocker.

"I need to find you some normal clothes," he said out loud. *And we need to stay out of sight for a while*, he thought to himself, and as soon as he thought it, he knew she heard him. *Yes, stay out of sight until I don't know when, maybe forever.* At least with women's clothes she might pass the suspicion test until they could get out of sight again.

They hopped back in the car, he buckled her up and they travelled south again. Her gaze didn't leave the water, that is, until the road veered away and the lake was blocked by homes and trees.

They passed through South Tahoe City, and her attention went to every nook and cranny in the little boutique town. Restaurants and bars, and clothing stores, sporting goods and small hotels and more bars.

Bob kept driving, the town was too busy to stop anywhere. Finally, at the edge of town, when he had just about given up hope, there he saw the store he was looking for. Tucked in between a bookstore and a coffee bar was a one door shop with a little yellow flower over the tiny window out front, and under the flower was a sign that read: The Daisy Bouquet Clothing Boutique.

He pulled over to a spot on the opposite side of the street and looked around. It was quiet here, with a just a few families and young couples walking around.

"You stay here, okay?"

She nodded.

"And put on these glasses." He pulled out the sunglasses from the center console and placed them gently on her face. "And keep the doors locked, okay?"

"What does that mean?" she asked.

"This is the door," he patted the door at his elbow. "You have one too. See?" And he pointed to her side of the car.

"Yes, but what is a 'locked'?"

He reached over her and pushed the little silver button down with his finger. "This is a lock to keep people out."

He could tell she was confused on the concept.

"Don't you have locks for your doors on your planet?"

She shook her head. "No."

He bit his lower lip. Of course there were no locks on her planet. Why would they need them? If you could read someone's mind and everyone always asked permission to do anything, there would never be a need to lock someone out. It would be like locking yourself out. But they weren't on her planet, they were on this one, and things were a little different here.

"Don't worry, you'll get used to it," he said. "Just stay here, okay?"

She nodded and smiled.

When he opened the door to the clothing store a little bell rang and an old lady looked up from the sewing machine at the back of the store.

"Can I help you?"

"Why yes, I'm here to buy some clothes."

The old woman scrunched her eyes while looking at him as though she didn't understand a single word that he'd just said.

"You sell clothes here don't you?" Maybe he should shout out his question since she was far away and hard of hearing. Or, maybe he'd walked into the wrong store after all, maybe they just repaired clothes and he'd read the sign wrong, but there along both walls were rack upon rack of dresses, and blouses and other types of obvious women's clothing which he had no idea what they were called.

"Why yes we sell clothes, it's just that…" Her voice trailed off as she got up from her chair, adjusted her glasses again and walked towards the front of store to have a better look at him.

"It's just that…" She muttered again to herself and squinted to see exactly what she was looking at. "It's just that, well…"

We could be here all day, thought Bob, and then he realized what her problem was, and he held up his hands, palms facing her while shaking his head in denial. Maybe she thought he was a cross dresser and was here to buy clothes for himself.

"Whoa now," he said with self-assurance. "I'm here to buy clothes for my…"

And then he had a mental lapse. Buy clothes for his what? His alien from another planet?

His brain froze and his eyes grew big, like a deer's eyes when confronted by the headlights from a Mack truck in the middle of a moonless night on the I-99. He struggled to find his tongue and then remembered where it was in the middle of his mouth.

"I'm here to buy clothes for my girlfriend," he finally said with confidence. And he pursed his lips and nodded crisply for the exclamation point on that profound statement.

She frowned then laughed while slapping her thigh. "Sure you are buddy, look it's none of my business who you buy your clothes for. What size do you… I mean, your girlfriend wear?"

Bob's face turned beet red, then he sighed while

shaking his head, utterly defeated. Now he had to tell her the worst part and he prepared himself to be totally humiliated.

"She's actually just about my size, to be honest."

The woman nodded. "Uh huh. Well come this way." She motioned to the middle of the store. "Size five and half."

Bob picked out a blouse and a pair of slacks and brought them to the cash register.

"Don't you want some underwear with that?"

"I guess."

"What size bra does she wear?"

"I don't know…" He cupped both his hands over his breasts, and she nodded.

"C-cup." She reached behind the register for a bra and a pair of panties and put them in a bag with the other items and punched in the numbers. "Seventy-seven ninety- five."

Bob handed over a hundred-dollar bill and waited for his change. The woman pulled out a black light, shining it on the bill front and back, ran her fingers over the edges feeling for the texture of the paper, and finally satisfied that it was legitimate, handed him twenty three one dollar bills and a nickel.

"Sorry, I'm all out of bigger bills," she said.

Bob frowned, then carefully folded the wad of money, put it in his wallet and picked up the package. His mood began to change from timid to overly self-confident. He would show this seamstress what was what. He strutted towards the front of the store.

"I want you to come over to the window and look across the street," he said. "Sitting in my car is the most beautiful woman in the world, and these clothes will only make her more beautiful, of that I'm sure."

She shrugged her shoulders and reluctantly followed him. He pointed out the plate glass window at his little blue car with the most beautiful woman in the world. There it was and there she was, and both were surrounded by over two dozen greasy muscled bikers with boots, chains, cigarettes and tattoos, and crooked smiles as they gazed down at the passenger seat of the car. There behind the shadow of the windshield he could see Reva gazing back at them.

"You were right," said the woman. "She really must be a beauty to attract that much attention that quickly, you've only been in this store about ten minutes." She turned to see his reaction, but Bob was already out of the door, half-running, half-jogging across the street.

Anger, jealousy, fear, and animal instinct all came to a boil in his mind as he got closer to the car. All lucid thought left him, and he became a seething volcano of violent emotion.

The biggest, meanest looking biker was leaning over the hood with his elbows on the windshield, staring down into the car at Reva. He looked like a size fifty, three hundred pounds, wearing an oily torn sleeveless leather jacket with the club's name stitched across the back that read 'Crack Heads'. There were skull and crossbones tattoos on his bald head, a giant rusted chain that he could tow a car with around his shoulders, a pair of num-chuks in his back pocket, and steel toed boots on his feet. The other two dozen hoodlums ranged around the car like a pack of hyenas circling a kill on the plains in Africa, and although smaller, were no less dirty and threatening. They were all looking through the windows at Reva with hungry eyes.

'I'll have to fight every one of them,' thought Bob, and prepared himself to die.

Reva caught sight of him, looking through a tiny opening in the car's windshield under the giant's armpit. Her face beamed when she saw him, he could hear her voice in his head, calm and soothing, as though she were singing a child's lullaby, and then all of the biker's eyes swiveled towards him as one pack of animals, red bloodshot eyes set within square jawed, bearded tough guy faces. They were all smiling too, as though they were in a happy little boy trance.

Bob stopped in his tracks and dialed back on his own aggressive attitude when he saw how non-aggressive they were. Maybe he wouldn't have to die today after all.

"Hey buddy," said the biggest meanest biker pulling his elbows off the windshield and standing huge and menacing and yet smiling down at Bob. "She sure is nice. Is she your girlfriend?"

At that instant Reva's mind was connected to Bobs and he could sense her wonder at the question. What did it mean?

I'll tell you what it means, thought Bob. It means you and I are a pair now, we belong together. We're friends. And since you're a...a...

The giant was waiting patiently for an answer, and Bob finally nodded. "Why yes, she is my girlfriend."

The giant reached out his bear paw and when Bob took hold of it, the giant shook it gently.

"Well you sure are lucky pal. She sure is wonderful."

The word resonated in the air, wonderful.

How such a word could come out of such a grimy and cruel looking mouth was a miracle. Bob nodded and rescued his hand from the vice grip, pulling it back to safety and rubbed it until the circulation returned.

"Yes, she certainly is."

The giant biker placed two giant pinkies in the side of his mouth, whistled loudly and made a quick circle in the air with his forefinger. The pack of jackals yelped as they mounted their choppers, revved them into a staccato roar, then drove down the street. They were a pack of animals again, some of them veering into the sidewalks to scare the tourists, running them into the road, and into the storefronts. With a final blast of unmuffled exhaust, they slowly faded off down the road and into the distance.

Bob looked over at the clothing store and could see the old woman shaking her head and laughing at him.

He unlocked the car door, tossed the package in the back and settled into his seat. "I see you kept the door locked like I asked you," as he pointed to the button. "They might have kidnapped you and rode off with you on their handlebars."

She was puzzled so he envisioned the thought and she laughed.

They were angry inside, for they felt unloved and unwanted, she thought. *And I sang them a song, it's a song that we sing to children when they are sad and lonely, and they became happy again. They are friends now.*

"Friends? Those guys?"

She smiled and he frowned.

"Look, you have to be very careful who you talk to…" Then he reconsidered and re-phrased his statement. "You have to be careful who you transmit thoughts towards. Not everyone is nice on this planet, believe me."

Her face turned serious. "I'm sorry."

"What am I going to do with you? And don't say 'be friends.'"

He waited for her answer. He knew he was being mean but couldn't help it at that moment in time.

"Show me your world," she said.

She was right of course. When you have a visitor from out of town, you show them around your city, show them the sights. This was a special situation, he couldn't take her to the city, she'd draw too much attention, and it might not be some harmless band of cut-throat bikers. The next thing you know they'd be in custody with the CIA and neither of them would be seen again. Taken to some black ops hole in the ground in Area 51 and locked up forever.

He had to keep her under wraps if that was even possible. The bikers were attracted to her and swarmed the car even though she was just sitting there minding her own business. The day was long, and it would be nice to just check into a little motel and get a good night's sleep, but it was imperative that they get as far away from civilization as possible.

He thought long and hard, finally deciding to take her to the best place he'd ever been to in his life. Yosemite. When he was just a kid and in the Boy Scouts, they took a trip there with his troop, and camped for a whole week. It was over a hundred miles as the crow flies south of Tahoe. They had two ways to get there, backtrack up through Truckee and down through Sacramento, or go east down the mountain to the Nevada side and run along the desert and back up into the Sierra Nevada mountains near Mono Lake.

They could get lost in Yosemite, hike into one of the little cracks in the mountains and hide out for a while until they figured out what to do.

"Alright, let's get out of here." He started the car, pulled away from the curb, and headed down the road. They went east along Lake Tahoe Boulevard, through the meat of the city that was placed in between the lake and the ski slopes of Heavenly Mountain. It was a four-lane mini-freeway full of cars and trucks. Reva stared out the passenger side window, silently watching the sights.

They came to a three-way intersection, where the styles of buildings changed abruptly from Chateau-style roofs on small two- and three-story structures, to square monoliths twenty stories high, sharp clean gambling casinos with neon lights advertising cheap buffets. he dividing line was marked by a simple little green sign to the side of the traffic light that read NEVADA STATE LINE.

Bob suddenly had a great idea, and his eyes got wide as he imagined it out loud.

"We could make a fortune," he said. He could barely speak, his voice quiet and tinged with excitement. "We could break the casino bank."

His mind whirled, drifted, pinwheeled around a single thought. Easy money.

"I have two hundred in cash right here in my pocket and we can parlay that into millions, right here, right now."

He pounded the palm of his hand on the steering wheel for effect. He looked over at Reva whose eyes also got wide as she mirrored the excitement that she felt from his thoughts. "We can be rich," he said.

Her breathing increased as she tried to realize what he was thinking, but no matter what it was, the feeling was nirvana. They could be rich. Whatever that meant.

"I'll set myself up at a little seven card stud, a poker game for the working class, one of the small tables, twenty-dollar ante, hundred-dollar limit.

You'll sit somewhere to the side, anywhere actually, just as long as you can see me and the other people in the game. You'll be able to read their minds, you'll know what their cards are, know what they're thinking, what they're going to wager on their hands, and you can relay that to me. I'll stall between bets so you can get the info to me, and we'll run the table, time after time, and they won't know what hit them! We'll build up our pile of cash then move onto a bigger table, hundred-dollar ante, thousand-dollar limit, and run that table into the ground. And then we'll move onto the biggest table in the joint, with no limit." His eyes grew wide.

The traffic light turned green like money, and he stepped gently on the gas, moving ever so slowly forward across the intersection and suddenly they were in Nevada. The gambling mecca of the universe.

Greed is like an invisible uncaring heartless and pitiless machine that can creep up and take over the most careful and honest of flesh and blood men if they're not constantly on guard.

And money is the grease that makes the wheels of that machine go round and round and roll right over those same men.

They were surrounded by giant casinos on either side of the road and Bob could almost hear the jackpots ringing and chips pouring across velvet green tables into his pockets.

He anxiously searched for a place to pull over, but the side of the road was blocked by pedestrian guardrails that went forever, intended to let the walking gamblers travel freely from Casino to Casino without being mowed over by desperate gamblers like himself.

I need to pull over so I can plan this out, he thought. *Why, it's foolproof. I'll devise a card counting method, after all, I'm a trained statistician, it can't be that hard. Then Reva can relay what the other players are seeing in their hands, and away we go.*

Away we go is right, he suddenly thought, as he envisioned both he and Reva dressed in orange jumpsuits, handcuffs being slapped onto their wrists and ankles, herded into a crowded five story prison with thousands of crazed tattooed inmates yelling from their cages and rattling the steel bars. He imagined the sound of the jail door slamming shut with a sickening clang.

Away we go to prison. Sure, it was foolproof.

Reva hid her face in her hands as Bob's thoughts trickled into her mind.

Being rich was fun but being in prison was a nightmare. Even so, prison would be the better of two evils if they ever got caught cheating a casino out of their money. If they got caught by the gangsters, they might get their fingers broken one by one with pliers in the basement.

Reva pushed her face deeper into her hands.

"Aw, never mind," said Bob as they passed the entrance to a Casino on his right and kept driving. "I'd rather be poor and free and still in one piece.

What about you?"

Reva pulled her hands from her face and nodded.

Greed is a heavy machine, but fear outweighs it.

11.

It was late in the afternoon and here on the East side of the Sierra mountains the sun set early, blocked by the craggy granite peaks to the west, as Bob and Reva drove down the mountainside.

They needed to find a campsite, or at least a spot on the side road where they could park and spend the night.

He pulled over onto a dirt road with no markings, rumbling over a small hill then down the other side of it, winding around a bend and through the forest of trees. Down and around a hairpin turn they went, the road rough and bumpy with dirt and rocks. Bob slowed down to a crawl to negotiate around a wheel-sized rock that must have rolled down the hillside from the mountain top above, but he didn't see the pothole the size of a bathtub on the other side of the rock. The front right tire and the entire front right side of the car dipped into the crevasse and they stopped with a thud.

The back tire, the one that provided the traction, was jackknifed in the air and barely making contact with the road. Bob gunned the engine and the tire spun, whirring on the dirt, creating a dust geyser behind them.

He put it in reverse and gunned the engine again. The geyser of dust from the spinning wheel surrounded the car and blocked the sun with a swirling brown cloud. "C'mon!" he shouted. "You bastard!" But the only result of his cursing was that Reva hid her face again, and he felt like a jerk.

They were stuck. He turned the engine off and waited until the dust cloud dissipated enough that he could open the door and assess the situation.

"I'm sorry Reva, I lost my temper."

"You were yelling at the dust, and it would not answer you. It's like yelling at the wind."

"Sometimes a guy just has to yell."

"It makes you feel better?"

"In a way, I suppose."

She smiled and took a deep breath. "You bastard!" she half yelled with a timid voice and then shrugged her shoulders.

He laughed and shook his head. "Girls shouldn't yell, or curse. C'mon, let's see what we've gotten into."

It was ugly. The boulder that they'd driven around must have acted like a backwater on a river, and when a recent rainstorm sent water cascading down the dirt road, it formed an eddy on the other side of it, the water carving out a hole that now held the little blue car captive, the entire front right corner dipped down into the crater resting against the edge of the pit, the bumper was dented and the headlight cracked and broken. The hole was so deep that the front tire was still suspended in the air, and when he looked at the back-left tire, it too was suspended and barely touching the dirt. They would need to lift the front end of the car to get enough traction on the back wheel in order to get out.

"We need a tow truck," said Bob as he kicked at the dirt. "Fat chance one's going to come along any time soon." Then he remembered the dire condition of his finances. "And if I do call for help it'll take my last dime to pay them."

Birds whistled in the trees and the branches rustled with the light wind. His mood calmed as he noticed that Reva was not paying attention to him or to the condition of the car but was completely focused on the scene around them. She cocked her head sideways as she listened for the source of the whistling, and her eyes searched the treetops. The wind and the trees didn't care about the car that was stuck in the hole and all the bird cared about was the notes in the song that it was singing.

Bob went and stood next to her, also searching for the source of the melody.

"There," he pointed. High in a tall juniper sierra was the source of the singing, he could barely make out its tiny shape: brown with tinges of white on its breast. "It's a sparrow, singing for its mate. Or in hopes of one."

On cue the bird whistled, and the song drifted down to them. It was a slow, light whistle that warbled through a soft midsection and ended with a high note. It fluttered its wings and waited for a response. Reva pursed her lips and began to whistle back, and Bob, for the life of him, could not tell the difference between bird and alien.

The poor sparrow was also fooled and looked around for the source of the song, and as Reva continued with the slow warble ending with an identical high note, the bird homed in on the direction of the sounds, and flew down and latched onto a lower branch right above them and waited.

"How did you do that?" Asked Bob.

"Do what?"

"Mimic that bird."

"I was just repeated its song."

"Well, you have a new friend," said Bob. Then he wondered quietly if she could also read its mind.

"No," she out loud. "I can't read its thoughts since they are so different than mine, but I can sense its feelings, they are simple, pure, basic and colorful, unimpeded by worry about the past or the future, intertwined with both song and shape, it is hungry and lonely and is calling out for its friend that is somewhere nearby. It felt joy when I returned its call, and it's now curious though wary of what I might be. I can mimic its sounds in perfect pitch and cadence, but I can't decipher the exact meaning."

The little bird began to sign again, slowly at first and building up steam, a slightly different song, and ended again on a crisp high note. When it was silent and waiting for an answer, another bird high in the treetops sang in reply, and the sparrow flew quickly off and disappeared.

Reva turned her attention to the car.

It was a strange thought and Bob couldn't discount the feeling of its importance as he watched her. She was locked into some sort of trance, not of a 'nirvana be at one with the universe' sort, but a problem-solving trance. She was looking for a solution to the car in the hole, he could see it in her eyes and her body language as she circled the car putting her hands on it and walking around it, feeling the mass and the structure and balance, studying the front bumper lodged tightly against the edge of the pit, mentally weighing the options. She walked to the back end and pointed down.

"This wheel propels the vehicle?"

"Yes."

She walked back to the front. "And this wheel is for the steering control."

It was more of a statement than a question, yet he still answered her.

"Yes."

She walked towards the woods and he followed her. Hundred-foot pines towered over them, and she stopped at one that had the circumference of a small house.

"What are you doing?" he asked her. She had a look of amazement on her face.

"We had these on our planet before the gamma rays destroyed the ozone. She wrapped her arms as around it as she could and placed her cheek against it.

"It's called a tree," he said. "This is a pine tree; the interior is fibrous and very hard. We build our homes from the wood on the inside of it."

She knocked on it, then peeled some bark from it, smelled it, then tasted it.

"That part, however, is soft, and we normally don't eat it."

Loggers had been through the area within the last year, and there were giant piles of branches nearby.

First the loggers cut down the tree, then cut off all the side branches before loading the giant logs onto a truck and hauling them to the mill. Most of the branches were smashed to little bits when the tree came crashing down, but there were still plenty of eight- to ten-foot craggy branches, wide as a burly wrestler's arm, stacked in the pile. he began to pull them out and laid them side by side until there ten in a row, and then she picked out three that were the same length and set them farther on the side. Then she picked thinner branches from the pile and also laid them side by side until there were nine and laid them with the other three larger branches.

"Let's bring them," she said and pointed to the car.

His mind was a blank question mark, and she

answered simply.

"You'll see."

And one by one they piled the long branches next to the front bumper of the car.

"I can see where this is heading," said Bob. "We're not going to be able ride out of this hole with these little sticks. The car weighs over two thousand pounds and will snap these twigs like toothpicks."

Reva pointed to the belt on Bobs waist.

"Do you have any more of those?"

He shook his head. "No, but I have some rope." He went around to the back of the car and retrieved a coil of thick rope from the trunk and brought it to her, then took off his belt and handed that to her as well.

She lay the belt and the rope on the ground four feet apart, then laid two little sticks across them and then one little stick on top making a sort of triangle. Then she put two of the bigger sticks next to the formation that held them tight, and then a big stick on top for another triangle, then three little sticks on one side of the big stick triangle.

"Hold these in place," she said.

Bob did as he was told, then she placed three more little sticks on the other side of the big stick triangle. "And here too," she said.

Again, Bob did as instructed, then she took the belt, wound it across the formation of big and little sticks, looped it through the buckle and latched it tight, then took the rope and tied an intricate loop knot and pulled it tight as well.

"The little ones will add to the big ones' strength. It's like a family. Little ones on their own will break under stress, and the big ones protect them. The little ones also protect the big ones and give them support. This is how it is on our planet."

"A force multiplier," said Bob while nodding in approval. "But the fact remains that this car literally weighs more than a ton, and there's no way that you and I will be able to jackknife it out of this hole with a stick, I don't care how family-strong it is."

She smiled and walked back into the forest and returned with a small two-foot-long log, half the width of a telephone pole, and set it in down in front of the bumper. Then using the little sharp stick, she dug a hole right in front of the bumper that was interestingly as wide as their stick contraption.

"Help me," she said. She motioned to the big stick and they muscled it up and stuck it down into the gap between the bumper and the edge of the pit. Now the big stick was wedged at a forty-five-degree angle up and away from the car, eight feet in the air with two feet of it under the car. She nestled the little log against the bottom part of the stick, then reached up and pulled down on the top of the stick.

Bob had a bit of a smirk on his lips and shook his head. Not a chance, and then his mouth fell open as he witnessed the front of the car lift up with a bit of a creak from the bumper, not much, just an inch or so, but it moved. He hustled over next to Reva and pulled down on the stick, which was bending slightly in the middle but holding together. With both of their strength together, they leveraged the car into the air using the log as a fulcrum.

The back-rear tire was nestled snugly on the ground.

"Drive the car backwards," said Reva.

"But how…" Bob wondered, and in his mind he could see the car rolling backwards, while the stick, which was leveraged against the log, rolled forward on it as the car retreated. He jumped into the driver's seat, started the engine, put it in reverse, and slowly backed away from the hole. Reva held the end of her magnificent customized stick and walked forward with it until the end of it hit the other side of the pit and the car was free.

Bob put it in park, turned off the engine and walked over to Reva, clapping his hands.

"You're an engineer."

"Sometimes the simplest solution is also the best and the easiest to accomplish."

"That was not simple."

He held out his arms and she walked towards him and pressed her chest against his and put her head on his shoulder, both of them gently wrapping their arms around each other.

All was calm.

Bob held his arms around her and rested his head on top of hers.

Time stood still.

For Bob, a simple act such as this with a woman would normally lead to an intimate situation, but this transcended that, and felt like the most natural thing in the world to do.

He didn't want or need to move and nearly sighed as everything relating to his ego vanished. There was no desire, anticipation, questions, fear, or need for anything in this world other than to stand there in an embrace.

She felt soft and comfortable, both in body and mind, and then the moment slowly passed, and they parted, Reva with a shy, knowing look his way.

"It's getting dark," said Bob. "We'd better get this car off the road in case someone comes barreling around the corner and knocks us into the hole again. He looked over at the empty clearing on the other side of the rock. We might as well just park there for the night. He drove the car around the rock and the hole and put the car in park in the center of the clearing. Then, he began gathered sticks and wood for a fire.

The temperature cooled with the setting sun, the light turning amber with deep dark shadows in the deep forest around them.

Reva sat on a log and began to weave her hair with bunched strands into a long ponytail that lay against the front of her right shoulder. She was watching the trees and the clouds and listening to wind while singing a soft tune with strange lilting sounds. She opened her mind and Bob studied her as he sat on a large boulder with a flat top.

It was a song about a small companion, an animal that lives on her planet. It was a friend that followed her everywhere, faithful, true, kind and humble, giving her comfort and calming the vibrations of her heart. It followed her everywhere, but it couldn't follow her here to this strange planet so far away from her home. It was her protector.

"What is that song you sing?" he asked.

"I sing for my Chalalabon. It is small and sweet with light soft fur. I cuddle it in my hands and nestle with it next to my ear to hear its heartbeat. It sleeps in the day and I care for it, and while I sleep at night it cares for me."

"How does it care for you while you sleep?"

"There is a small predator on our planet. Cunning and secret with sharp teeth that slithers in the dark and lives and hides in holes and tunnels deep in the ground. While animals sleep at night, it creeps upon them and takes little bites. Then, it hides, bites and hides. Its teeth are so sharp and small that you can't feel it's bites until it is too late. My chalalabon, my protector has night vision, it can see heat, and while the evil creature has blood that runs colds in its veins. My protector can see the pinpoint light in the middle of its eyes, and it pounces on the evil one and devours it whole while I sleep peaceful and safe. I sing for it, as it is now alone with no one to protect, or to protect it. And I am also alone."

"I can be your protector."

She laughed. "You are not furry and small."

"I can grow a beard."

She laughed again at the visual.

"Don't you have houses?" Bob asked, "Where you can close and lock the door to keep the slithering menace out?"

"Of course. We have magnificent houses for the babies and the old people, and for those that are sick and injured and healing, and for everyone in the times of wind and rain, but we all sleep outside because that is how we stay in contact with the one who created us. However, you must tell me again what is a lock? I don't understand the concept."

Of course you wouldn't, thought Bob.

"You have slithering things that hide in dark places and come out at night, and we have bad people with those same traits. Since we don't have the Chalalabon, we use locks to keep them out."

Bob decided they would sleep on the floor of the forest, rather than try to scrunch into the back seat of the car. He picked out a worthy-looking spot with a ready-made bed of pine needles.He grabbed an extra armful of soft needles for good measure and piled them up until he had a king-sized mattress half a foot high. He smoothed the high points until it was nearly flat, then went to the car for the towels and blanket to share.

He rolled one towel into a tight cylinder for himself, and the other in a loose tube for Reva. He set the two makeshift pillows next to each other and, now for the test, gently laid down on the pine cushion. It was the most comfortable bed he'd laid on in two days. He was careful not to scurry the fine work he'd done as he pulled half the blanket over his feet and tucked it under his chin.

He patted the pine needles next to him and smiled up at Reva.

"You will sleep next to me. I give you permission."

She smiled at that, and he chuckled.

"Why do you laugh?" she asked.

"I think it's kind of cute, always asking for permission."

"This is the right thing to do."

"Maybe someday," he said, "if we're lucky and can stay together for a long time, you won't need to ask for permission. You'll know that it's already been given."

Straight above, through the branches of the high pine trees, even though the sky had a tinge of blue remaining, the first stars of the night twinkled in the clear mountain air.

As dusk and darkness began to deepen around them, Bob picked up the computer pad that was lying next to him and turned it on. In the corner of his eye he could see Reva watching him. With his finger he pressed on a link that took him to a page with hundreds of links. Then he pressed one, pulling up a book, and with quick swipes found the pages he was looking for.

Continuing where they left off, he read to Reva

again from the book of world literature. The last part of the Homer's Odyssey, where Odysseus returning home from the Trojan war finds his home over-run with young strong braggarts without a clue as his identity, and slays them all, bringing upon him the wrath of entire island of Ithaca and a final battle that nearly cut every man to the ground, that is, until the goddess Athena and a thunderbolt from Zeus ended the fighting and brought peace to the land.

When that story was through, he continued with Hamlet and the treachery of Laertes, the poisoned cup and the poison tipped rapier blades that killed them all.

The darkness had completely surrounded them when he clicked on the encyclopedia of world events and read the details of World War One, the twenty-two million dead, wounded, and missing in action, the trenches and the mustard gas, Sergeant York, the armistice and the League of Nations. Then he skimmed through World War Two with fifty million dead over six years, the Nazi invasion of Europe and Russia, D-Day and the invasion of Normandy, the Battle of the Bulge, and the firebombing of Dresden. Then he read about the nuclear bombings, first of Hiroshima and then Nagasaki, that brought the war to a terrifying conclusion.

"And it not over," he continued. "We have new wars, little ones, that are always popping up. In the middle east, lands far away from here, we have wars in Syria, Iraq, Afghanistan, where armies are positioned against each other."

"And that's not everything," he thought. "In every major city in our country, shootings happen every day. Chicago, Detroit, Seattle. Plus, there are some in any small town you can name, too."

She was frightened, he could sense it. Still, he needed to continue.

"These are things you should know about us," he said. "The worst of the worst." He felt as though a stone wall had been suddenly erected between them.

"Isn't there anything good in your past, or your present?" She shielded her eyes from his with her hand, fearful that he would have nothing to say.

"Of course, I just thought you should hear about the foulest, most deficient and regretful part of humanity, the bottom of the pit so to speak, and then we can build up on that. I have one more to read to you. The oldest one of all."

Genesis.

He read her the first three pages detailing the first seven days of creation, Adam and Eve living in the perfect world in the Garden of Eden. Then came the apple and the serpent, the fig leaves to cover their nakedness, God's wrath and fury, their expulsion from the comfort of the garden into the wild. Then placing fierce winged angels, the cherubim, at the entrance to the garden with a flaming sword.

He continued on with the first two sons, describing the lives of Cain and Abel, two brothers, the farmer and the shepherd. "You see, Cain killed

Abel, and that is the curse that we all still carry."

The sky was now completely black, and the stars were filling the sky to the east.

"What about your people?" he asked. "What about your wars, and your battles?"

She took her hand away from her face and looked deep in his eyes.

"Our past is different than yours, nearly opposite. In the beginning there was constant strife and turmoil. Brother against brother. Family against family. It was the time of the great awakening. One day, a young boy was trapped in a well. He was struggling to keep his head above the water and would soon die. He didn't have the strength to cry out for help and called out to his mother with his mind with the last bit of his strength. His mother who was nearby working in the field, felt the prayerful cry, felt her son's presence in her mind, and with her heart bending the universe to her will called back to him and brought him out of the well and to her side in an instant. When God found out that she was able to hear her sons' thoughts and bring him through space, he brought us out of the wilderness and into the garden. For if we could hear each other's thoughts and could travel through space, there was nothing we couldn't do."

"No war? No battles? No brother against brother, sister against sister?"

"Of course not. How could you when you can feel what the other is feeling? If you would hurt someone, you would also be hurting yourself. You would feel their pain as though it was happening to you."

"Everything was perfect."

"Yes, and then the supernova happened."

She was silent for a moment and then continued.

"We think it happened to test us."

Bob turned off the pad and it was suddenly pitch black around them, the stars shining far away in the sky above.

Reva was quiet lying next to him, he turned his head to see if she was sleeping. Her eyes were opened wide, watching the stars. Maybe she was worried, he thought, about the darkness, about the story about the serpent in the Garden of Eden, or maybe she was worried about being here without her beloved Chalalabon.

"You can scoot closer to me," he said. "I'll protect you."

12.

For a moment he felt her warm shoulder and the side of her hipbone gently pressing against his, while a soothing song surrounded him from her mind, like angel wings gently strumming a harp, and the next thing he knew, he was blinking his eyes and looking up at the first grey light of morning that filled the forest.

In the back of his mind, he somewhat recalled sleeping, but it was all a blur. His back was a little achy and he sat up, rubbed his face and looked next to him. Reva was gone. then He spotted her sitting on a log nearby, watching him.

She smiled as he shook the cobwebs out of his head and rubbed his eyes again.

"What happened?" he asked.

"You were sleeping like a baby."

"All I remember was a song."

"That's the song we sing to babies to lull them to sleep. It works with you also."

"You can say that again."

"Who's Sara?" she asked.

Bob eyed her with suspicion. He hadn't thought about his ex-girlfriend in two days, not since Reva had suddenly appeared. He'd actually forgotten all about her, and the break-up on that fateful morning.

"Why do you ask about her?"

"You were saying her name in your sleep."

Bob was suddenly worried, and his suspicions doubled. "Were you reading my mind, reading my dreams while I was sleeping?"

She laughed. "Of course not, I wouldn't be able to do such a thing without your permission. And besides, it's impossible. You have to be conscious for our minds to blend, and dreams are when the mind is unconnected to the body, in a way, it's when the mind is on vacation and able to go wherever it wants."

"Do you have dreams?"

"Of course. Dreams are fun, most of the time. Especially if you can have a tiny bit of control over them."

"Sometimes I have dreams where I can fly," said Bob. "Arms outstretched high above the countryside like a bird or a superman. And sometimes I have dreams where I don't need to walk. I can slide with my feet on the ground, with perfect balance, feet sliding on the road or the sidewalk, and then lifting slightly in the air and gliding. It's so easy, it seems so real that when I wake up, it's as though it wasn't a dream."

They were silent for a moment, then Bob felt the need to explain.

"Sara was my girlfriend for a while," he said. "For a few months anyways. We had fun together, or so I thought, and then suddenly a couple of days ago, she broke it off with me, 'broke up with me' is how we say it here on Earth. That's why I came up here to the mountains, to get away from it, from the feeling of being abandoned."

Reva walked over and sat next to him. She placed her hand lightly on his shoulder.

"If you were truly together, you could never be broken up as you say. You could never be abandoned."

"I guess if all that never happened, you'd never be here with me now."

Her wide black eyes gazed at Bob. "You asked me if I ever have dreams."

"Yes."

"I dreamed of you."

The wind whispered through the trees as they watched each other. He felt himself slowly being drawn into her calm, velvet eyes.

She continued. "Three nights ago I dreamed of you. There was a large city with tall glass buildings. I saw you walking through a crowd of people. I could see their faces, they were angry and agitated. They were yelling at you, yet their voices were silent, the only sound I could hear was the sound of your beating heart. The angry crowd was pulling at you with their hands, trying to hold you back. And yet you kept walking forward, you escaped their grasps, and kept walking straight out of the city and into the wilderness. You were sad and lonely, I couldn't see your face, but I could see the inside of your heart."

Tears were running down her cheeks, and Bob felt moisture welling up in the corners of his own eyes.

"You were lonely and were walking towards me, I was waiting on the side of a mountain with the stars circling overhead, yet you could not see me. I tried to shout out your name so you would see me, but I didn't know who you were. And suddenly I was afraid that you would never see me waiting and would pass by in the night and be lost forever."

He frowned and decided to change the subject. "You must be hungry, I know I am." He walked over to the car, opened the trunk and rummaged through the food box. He came back with two plastic baggies and sat back down next to her.

"Hold out your hand."

She complied, and he poured out a mixture of nuts and raisins from the first baggie, then poured an equal amount in his own hand and stuffed the pile in his mouth, watching her as he chewed. She was cautious and studied the items, poking them with her fingers, the nuts were hard and covered in salt and the raisins soft and squishy.

"What?" she was confused.

"It's called trail mix."

Hesitantly at first, she took one of each and placed

them on her outstretched tongue, retracted it, then began to chew. Her face brightened and she exhaled with delight and ate the whole handful.

"Thank you."

"Peanuts and cashews and raisins, they grow on vines mostly, one is a seed and other is a fruit. That was just the first course. Here at Chateau le Bob's Restaurant in Tahoe City we aim to please."

He opened up the next plastic baggie and handed her a long-blackened strip sprinkled with hardened bits of pepper.

"What's this?"

"Jerky. Try it, you might like it. This is the main course." He took a strip himself and nipped the end slowly chewing, while studying her from the corner of his eye.

She shrugged her shoulders and sniffed at it like an animal, unsure and alert of such a strange looking food. Then, she took a tiny nibble, her nose crinkling as she chewed. The corners of her mouth turned upside down in a frown.

"Don't you like it?"

"It tastes strange."

"It's beef jerky. Meat. From an animal we have on Earth called a cow."

The second that he said it he knew he'd made a mistake. Her eyes widened, while from his mind to hers the image of a large furry cow, mostly white with big black splotches down its sides, round ears, big wide loving eyes. She saw a carefree and happily animal chewing its cud in a green field with yellow flowers, while other cows mooed and chewed beside it.

She jumped up and ran to the forest, dry spitting and hacking as she went. Running swiftly to the nearest tree she could find and pulled the bark off, stuffing it in her mouth and scrubbing her tongue with it, scouring the awful taste of animal flesh away.

Her head hanging low, she sat with her back to the trunk and caught her breath while he jogged towards her with his palms high in the air.

"I'm sorry, I didn't know."

"You eat animals?"

"Well, not all the time."

"Living breathing creatures?"

"Um…"

"You take the life away from them? Or have they already died a natural death, and you merely transfer their essence into your system by eating their flesh?"

He sighed and sat down next to her. "I guess it's hard to explain, but to tell you the truth I don't really know for sure where this jerky came from. I don't even if it's from a cow. It could be from a pig or a horse or a donkey for all I know. It could be roadkill."

He saw a vision of an animal in the middle of the road next to the center stripe, flattened by a car's tire. He was making it worse.

"All I know for sure is I didn't make it myself, I just bought it from the shelf at a store." He tasted the jerky flavor still in his mouth. "They sure do make it easy for you to be an executioner."

In his mind he remembered a video he once saw that was made by an anti-animal cruelty group. Supposedly it was filmed inside a hot-dog factory and showed how they were made from beginning to end. No one really knew if it was true or not, but it was so gruesome, that after watching it, the question of whether or not it was true was irrelevant. The damage to a consumer's psyche was permanent.

The title was in bold red letters something along the lines of: "*You'll never want to eat a hot dog again after seeing this.*" Then you entered a rusting dilapidated building with the metallic sound of an apparatus that was grinding up little pigs, whole carcasses falling off the conveyor belt into the grinding gears of the machine, ears and noses, teeth and bones, hair and hooves, then cooking the gooey pink mixture in a giant boiling vat, finally pouring the contents through a round tube into little individual round sacks. It was horrible. He cringed just thinking about it.

"I'm an idiot."

She reached her hand out and put it on his shoulder for comfort.

"You are different from us."

"What do you eat? How do you stay alive? You must have nutrition," he said. "Don't tell me you eat the bark from the trees."

"The trail mix in the first bag. Seeds and fruits, they come from a plant. We have the same types of food on our planet, different in some ways but very much the same. A plant produces the food for us, and we nourish the plant in return. This is what we live on, and I am not here to judge you for what you eat. We too have been meat eaters, but that was long ago in our past, and we have moved away from all of that. I was just shocked for the moment, that is all."

"Well, if it's any consolation I tossed the jerky over there, and I we won't have it in our car." He pointed with his index finger to an area near the clearing where they'd slept. The little pile of jerky was being attacked by a small pack of birds battling over it, half a dozen black crows pecking and flapping their wings till every last morsel was devoured. Then, they strutted and cawed at each other while searching with their beady little eyes for any remaining crumbs before flying off into the sky in different directions.

"Those crows are definitely not vegetarians," said Bob. "If we stopped moving for long, they'd attack us like that jerky, in fact, just about every creature in this forest would do the same."

"That's what sets us apart from them."

13.

After the front end of the car went into the hole, the steering had become unaligned.

One of the tie rods must have gotten bent and now the car pulled to the right, just slightly and not all the time, but just enough to be annoying. Every now and then Bob had to nudge the wheel to bring the car back on line and into the center of the lane. He tried speeding up and slowing down but nothing worked, so he decided to go a little slower than the speed limit of sixty miles an hour, just in case something snapped and sent them into the oncoming traffic or the ditch running along the side of the road.

There was very little traffic at this early hour, right after sunrise, and the round bright globe to the east, unhindered by clouds, burned the fields beneath. It looked like it would be a merciless hot day at sea level in the lee of the shadow of the Sierra Nevada, the semi-desert shimmering with heat, the sun only two fists above the horizon and rising fast.

Bob kept to the right in the slow lane, not wanting to attract any attention, though sometimes that was the worst thing to do. He was carrying a passenger that might not be welcomed and understood by most of the inhabitants of this planet. Anything different and out of the ordinary was suspect, and to be shunned.

Stay within your own comfort zone and all would be well. 'Stranger danger' was taught early, often, and for good reason when a child is young and vulnerable. That rhyming lesson lingered inside everyone in the back of their consciousness whether they wanted it or believed it. Tt was imbedded in the bedrock of their being, ingrained like a little innocent pebble on the beach of awareness.

Bob kept to the slow lane. They would head south towards Bridgeport, and on past the southern edge of Mono Lake, then take Tioga Road up to the mountains, head west into Yosemite, and camp there until their stock of trail mix ran out. By then, he'd have a plan.

There was a car a half mile ahead of him and another one half a mile behind, and Bob was in his comfort zone for driving. The oncoming traffic was much heavier as travelers headed to the mountains and Tahoe.

A highway patrol car was in the fast lane in the opposite side of the road, and as they got closer to each other Bob noticed the driver's eyes lock onto his little blue car, then he swiveled his head as they passed each other.

Bob instinctively tried to keep his eyes straight ahead on the road in front of him, but he flinched. He couldn't see the patrol man's eyes as they were hidden behind mirrored sunglasses, but he felt his gaze going right through him.

He was definitely checking us out, thought Bob. His blood pressure went up, his breathing got shallow and he instinctively looked in the rear-view mirror, like a criminal running from the law.

He laughed nervously. "I haven't done anything wrong and yet I'm paranoid." Then, in the rear-view mirror he saw the patrol car do a U-turn and begin to follow them, gunning its powerful engine, dust billowing from the back end as it gathered speed. It was right on their tail in seconds.

In the rearview mirror, Bob could see two square-shouldered, square-jawed cops in brown khakis, both with mirrored sunglasses. Suddenly, blue lights lit up their world and the whoop of the sirens commanded them to pull over.

There was a small river running next to and below the grade of the highway with no guardrail to keep a car from plunging into it. Bob pulled over to the gravel side, careful to stay well away from the steep cliff that led to disaster.

He kept half an eye on the rear-view mirror and tried to appear innocent, not making any sudden moves to alarm the officers.

"I feel like I robbed a bank, or worse."

What's wrong? asked Reva with her mind. She could sense the alarm and danger.

"Just follow my lead and keep your sunglasses on, okay? These are police officers and they're our friends. There's nothing to worry about."

"Then why are *you* worried."

"I'm always worried. You'll get to know that about me, if we're lucky enough and stick together long enough."

"This is different."

He couldn't lie to her anymore to make her feel at ease. Heck, he could never lie to her anyways, she could read his mind.

"Remember back in Tahoe when I had that little idea about going into the casino and using you to cheat at cards?"

She nodded, the thought was painful.

"Remember my vision about being handcuffed and thrown into prison?"

She nodded again, slower this time, wary of what was coming.

"Well, these are the guys that put the handcuffs on people. We have to be just a little bit careful right now, okay?" He winked at her to help her relax. "Just stay calm and we'll be alright."

He rolled down the driver's side window and smiled up at the officer who did not smile back. The palm of the cop's right hand was resting on the handle of his service revolver, which was holstered on his hip and was clearly unlatched.

"Good morning sir," said the officer politely while continuing to rest his hand on the gun.

Bob tilted his head slightly, trying to hear the inflection in the tone of the policeman's voice. It was a southern California accent with a very slight southern drawl on the edges.

"Good morning," replied Bob. His cheerful smile waning as he watched the grim face of the patrolman.

"I pulled you over because I noticed that your front right headlight is broken, and that is a safety hazard."

"Oh, right," Bob chuckled nervously. "You see officer, I parked a little too close to a rock last night up in Tahoe. I'll get a replacement right away. I can guarantee you that I won't be driving at night until I do."

"License and registration please."

The other officer was standing next to the passenger side window and looking straight down at Reva and the glove box that Bob opened to remove the registration. His wallet was in the center console and he carefully removed the license and handed the two documents to the officer, who took them without looking down at them. He was still observing Bob and Reva, he seemed especially interested in Reva.

"Good morning ma'am," he said to her and waited for a reply.

Bob realized what the cop was doing. He was waiting for a response to see if she had an accent, to see if she was a foreigner.

Maybe he didn't pull them over to check on a broken headlight, maybe he pulled them over to see if his passenger was an illegal alien. *You bastard*, he thought, *you have no idea how right you are.*

The officer leaned closer since Reva did not answer him right away. He lowered his sunglasses on his nose so that his vision was unimpaired. His eyes were brown, the edges crinkled with suspicion.

"Are you okay ma'am?"

Bob reached out to Reva with his mind. *Say these words to him*, thought Bob. *But keep your sunglasses on.*

Why yes, good morning, he thought, adding a southern belle inflection to his relayed tone of voice.

Reva leaned over towards Bob and smiled sweetly at the officer. "Why yes good morning."

The officer beamed slightly. "Is that a southern accent I notice?"

Why yes, I'm from Georgia, thought Bob with a little extra sugar in the intonation. Reva repeated it exactly.

"I knew it," smiled the officer, and took his hand off the gun. "I'm from Alabama," his southern drawl bubbled to the top and overwhelmed his California accent. "Why heck, we're practically neighbors."

The officer handed the license and registration back to Bob without ever having looked at them and tipped the brim of his cap.

"Have a nice day folks, and don't forget about that headlight sir."

They sat there for a while after the police car left

and watched the traffic go by, the whoosh of a car or a truck and then silence. Then another whoosh and silence.

The road that stretched into the distance ahead of them shimmered with heat waves from the mounting sun.

Bob was still shaken from being pulled over. He'd always had an imperceptible fear of being detained and thrown into prison, caged behind bars for the rest of his life.

"You probably don't have police on your planet, do you?"

She shook her head no.

"I didn't think so, why would you need them? No locks on your doors, no police. You probably don't have military forces either."

"What is that?"

"Standing armies, ready to go to war with guns and missiles. Remember the stories I read to you last night? World war one and two. The worst of the worst. Millions of people killed over little arguments?"

She hid her head in her hands, trying to forget what he told her the night before. After a moment she wiped a tear from her eyes and looked back at him.

"We do have forces of people trained to respond at a moment's notice, sort of like your armies in a way, only they don't kill each other, they help each other. Whenever there's a natural disaster, a storm, an earthquake, flooding." And then as an afterthought she added. "A supernova. You see we have armies of people ready to mobilize and work to fix whatever problem needs to be fixed."

"You're a funny sort of people, aren't you?"

They were silent for a moment.

Bob turned back towards Reva. "Those policemen who just pulled us over. Could you hear their thoughts?" he asked.

She nodded. "Very slightly. I knew you were worried and so I did not ask for their permission. But I could sense their anxiety. They were concerned about their safety first, and they were curious about us, why we were here, who we were. They were apprehensive, slightly scared, as one would be out in the wild at night without their Chalalabon to protect them from the quick biting teeth."

"What about the bikers back up in Tahoe, or the old man at the campground where we first met, or the people that we passed on the streets."

"Yes, I can feel their vibrations."

"What about the people passing by in these cars right now?"

"I can feel all the vibrations from all the people in a radius that is farther that we can see. Past the horizon, but not much farther than that."

"You feel their vibration. What does that mean?"

She was silent for a moment, thinking about how to put it into words so that it could be something that he could understand.

"You see the shimmering of the road ahead, and the desert around us?"

He nodded. "Those are heat waves rising from the surface. They distort the air, light bends at a different speed through the heat wave and makes it look like it's shimmering, makes the horizon look like it's water. People lost in the desert see the heat waves and think its water on the horizon, it's also called a mirage, but it's an illusion. They'll be lost in the desert without water, dying of thirst and losing their minds, then they see the mirage and run for it. But they never reach a drop of water."

"It's like that with me. The heat wave, the mirage is what I can feel. There are hundreds, and thousands of people in my range. I can sense their feelings the same way as we see these heat waves. There is like a core of happiness and contentedness, but on the edge I can sense a constant hunger, a worry about the future and regret about the past. I feel it coming from you also."

He bit his lip as he digested what she had just said. He reached over and took off her sunglasses, folded them onto the seat between them, and looked deep into her dark eyes.

"It's true what you say. I don't have much money, the future is cloudy and a little bit scary, and I have made many mistakes in the past. I carry them with me whether I want to or not. I guess that's a human trait, and if you're feeling that vibration all around us, then I'm not alone. I had a feeling I wasn't."

She smiled at that.

"Of course you're not alone. None of us are."

"What do you mean?"

"That shimmering that you see on the road?"

"Yes?"

"We can also feel the Creator."

His breathing stopped and he narrowed his eyes at her.

"You mean God?"

"Of course," she said

"Slow down."

"What's wrong?"

"My parents used to tell me that it was blasphemous to say you could hear God. He was so far above us puny little mortal beings, and in such a higher realm that there was no way that anyone in their right mind could ever hear him, and if anyone ever said they could, then they were either lying or possessed. They especially warned me about people in power, in the government who even slightly implied that whatever they intended to do, whatever act of the government they meant to impose on the population, was somehow inspired words of wisdom from the almighty."

She smiled slyly.

He twisted his mouth. "What?"

"You remember the old saying you told me up on the mountain last night?"

"Which old saying?"

"The one about someone not being able to see the forest for the trees?"

"Yeah?"

"This is the same thing."

"How?"

"You are so concerned about the future, and worried about the past, that you've lost sight of the present."

"Continue."

"There's an ever-present force in the Universe. It holds together the fabric of space and time. It's like a glue that you can't see. It's never the future, and it's never the past, but it's always a continuous, ever present… now. It's always now. And if you let go of the past and forget about the future, put those concepts behind you and sweep them out of your consciousness. If you slow down, quiet your mind and your entire being and listen to the now, the ever present incredible now, you'll see what I'm talking about. You have the ability, I know you do, but it's like not seeing the forest for the trees, you're preoccupied with the individual trees and you're missing the forest, which in this case is the glue that holds everything together which we call the Creator."

Bob shrugged his shoulders.

"Close your eyes for a moment Bob. Just feel the here and now and shed all the other thoughts from your mind. I'll be here with you and help you if you give me permission."

"Okay, I'll play along. I give you permission to take me along with you." He closed his eyes and waited. He tried to clear his mind. Nothing happened. He heard a whoosh as a car went by, and it wasn't God. Off in the distance and far from the car he heard the caw-caw of a crow and it also wasn't God.

Bob waited, and the silence around him grew larger and began to envelope him.

His memory was jolted in the quiet and his mind drifted back to when he was a child and his parents would take him to church when they were still alive. They'd dress him up in a little suit and tie, make sure Bob's hair was neat and combed, his shoes tied tight, and always arrive early to get good seats.

They'd sit in the front row to the left side of the altar, which was draped with the cloth. He was mesmerized by the two candles sitting on the front corners of the altar with the yellow flickering flames and the little stream of grey and black smoke that wound up, around, and through the air into the rafters high above them. While in the background and booming all throughout the hall, the clear voice of the priest and all the parishioners erupted in unison:

We believe in one God.

He measured the candles with his little thumb in front of his eye to see which one was taller.

The Father, the Almighty.

Then one day he noticed the air above the candles waffling, heat waves rising from the flame and changing the nature of the air above it. The heat waves blending the air into prisms that distorted the images behind them, melding the air in gentle, uplifting waves.

Maker of Heaven and Earth.

He imagined an invisible world in the air above the candle, a world that only he could see. Cascading upwards in magical colors and forms.

Of all that is seen and unseen.

It was a revelation to a small child of seven or eight, at the time he wondered what other strange things were unseen and un-noticed in the world around him, and over the long stretch of time that had passed he'd forgotten all about his revelation sitting in front of the church, and hadn't even thought about it for the past twenty years or so, until just now. It was in the past, he lived it, and remembered it, but it was gone in the blink of an eye.

Bob's mind whirled with the fond memory and as fast as that it was gone, and he was smack dab in the present. His heart beat loudly and the blood flowed quickly through his veins. His muscles were tensing and untensing, clear vibrant thought coursing throughout his entire body, which had become something like a giant pair of eyes and ears, heightened synapses, hearing all, feeling all around him. A tiny mote of dust floated slowly in front of his nose and he could sense its existence.

Effervescent as the color of a rainbow on the horizon, in the background of his mind he felt a tiny presence. It felt as though it was always there, and he just now noticed it, consumed by his ego and his wants and needs, he never realized the presence of something that was greater than all else, and he wanted to hide his face.

Humble, meek, as timid as a moth in a hurricane wind, he cringed inside with shame and fear. He wanted to run away and hide, he was not worthy to be here or to see this now, or ever. And then just as suddenly, he felt an overwhelming compassion, stillness, peace and calm wash over him and soothe his fears. A blanket of kindness.

He saw a golden glow at the edge of his being, gently touching the perimeter of his senses. The structure of it indiscernible, and infinite.

Everything was going to be okay.

That single thought reverberated throughout him, then permeated his entire being and he became one with it.

Everything was going to be okay.

A fourteen-wheel semi-truck passed by doing seventy-five and nearly sucked their little car into its vortex. The tiny car shuddered violently in all directions, shaking Bob out of his trance.

He grabbed the wheel and yelled while watching the steel square tail end of the truck pass by. In a cloud of dust, pebbles rained down on their windows and roof. The truck driver blasted his horn for good measure as it cleared. Bob's eyes were wide as saucers. And just like that, the car settled down and all was quiet again as though nothing had ever happened.

He saw God on the side of the road while a semi passed by at arm's length.

He remembered he needed to breathe, and sighed

instead, then took short relieved sips of air.

Everything was going to be okay.

Bob looked over at Reva, she still had her eyes closed, a peaceful look on her face, unperturbed by the death vehicle that had nearly crushed them. When she felt that his attention had turned towards her, she opened her eyes and smiled at him.

"Is this how it is with your religion?" she asked.

He shook his head, slightly embarrassed at his inequality. "Not even close."

"Now do you see what I was telling you?"

His lips trembled as he tried to answer. "Did I just see God?" His voice was just above a whisper as he said it.

"What we see is a glimpse, a small contact with the Creator. It is all we can handle with our simple state of mind and spirit. Maybe someday when we cross over to the other side we'll be able to enjoy a closer conversation, but for now this is the extent of our dialogue, which as you can see goes beyond words."

"You know this much." It was hard for him to ask the next question afraid of what the answer might be. "Do you know what happens when you die?"

Thankfully she shook her head in the negative. "Of course not. That is beyond our realm of understanding and perhaps for our own good. We have been provided with many gifts, but some things are best left unknown. It gives a living being something to strive for. Maybe someday we'll be able to sit next to the Creator in some way shape or form and have a discussion, that is our great hope, and for which we keep an open, humble mind and we always ask for permission in everything that we do. That one simple act is the core of our belief."

Bob looked back down the straight asphalt highway stretching out in front of them, the semi-tractor long gone and out of sight while the mirage remained, filtering waves of light that cascaded up towards the heavens.

He pulled back onto the highway and they continued driving south on the dusty highway.

14.

Reva watched through her window at all the wondrous sights, the bleak foothills of the Sierra to the right, and the bleaker flatlands to the left.

Millions of years of erosion had done no favors to this side of the range. While on the other side of the mountain, thousand-mile long cold fronts marched across the Pacific Ocean, gathering moisture and dumping it all in great swaths on the windward side. The wet side of the mountains enjoyed winter rains that enriched the soil, soaking and growing an abundance of plants and creating a lush rich multitude of soil. It was the breadbasket of the west coast.

However, this side, the leeward side, enjoyed no such luxuries. Any water that dropped from the sky quickly dissipated into the atmosphere. The water molecules leached salt up and out of the soil, leaving a crust on the surface to impede any but the hardiest plant growth.

Even so, here and there scattered along the river that wound its way south, were pockets of life. There were patches of dirt that over the millennium had collected enough water and plant growth to create a living compost of sorts that was suitable for some type of farming.

Bob spotted one such oasis and decided to stop for a breather. On the outskirts of a small farm was a mom-and-pop fruit stand bordering a small orchard with picnic tables in the shade next a tiny wandering stream.

They pulled into the gravel parking lot, the tires crunching on the pebbles. As they pulled up, they scanned the area.

A sign read 'Farm Fresh Produce' in front of a small store only a little bigger than the car they rode in with. An awning for shade and tables was set up with round colorful fruit and green vegetables. An old woman was busy dusting the windows, a job that would never be complete in this harsh environment.

"You see that little table over there?" asked Bob pointing to a green picnic table under a tree. "Why don't you go claim it, and I'll bring us some food to try."

Reva smiled, reached over, touched his arm gently, and got out of the car.

Bob took the computer pad and carried it, cradled under his arm, to the fruit stand while looking over the wares. There were pears and oranges, strawberries and tomatoes and every type of vegetable known to man. There were carrots and lettuce and peppers of every size and color.

"Good morning, sir," the old woman said, smiling widely. She finished her dusting and stood ready at the cash register next to the weight scale.

"Good morning ma'am, you've got all my favorites."

"Yes sir, we pick them fresh every day. Whatever is left over goes to the livestock."

Dave pulled some plastic bags off aa roll and struggled opening the first one until he found the trick of rubbing the palm of his hand with his fingertips. He placed two oranges in the first bag, two pears in the second, and then half a dozen strawberries in the third.

She still smiled as he handed her the bags to weigh and even though she was smiling, he could tell she was disappointed in the small purchase.

He reassured her. "We'll enjoy these in the shade, and I'll pick up some more before we leave."

Her smile widened. "Thank you, sir."

Sales must be slow next to the busy highway, Bob thought, *people scurry from one place to the next and are too busy to stop for a piece of fruit.*

Bob walked over to the little picnic table and sat down next to Reva. She had taken off her sunglasses and was literally beaming: the color of her cheeks rosy pink and dark black eyes sparkling at the sight of the fruit.

"What do you think about this?" he asked her.

"It is beautiful."

He put a strawberry in her hand and took one for himself. He took a bite and showed her the remaining half in his fingers.

"It's soft and sweet with just a tinge of tartness."

She carefully took a bite and winced, the muscles in her face contracting with the unfamiliar flavor.

"What do you think?"

Her reply was a universal one: a slight, low, "*Yuuuuummmm*" that purred and reverberated from under her cheekbones and out into the dry air.

They moved onto the orange, which he peeled. He showed her how to split the slices and retain the juice until they popped them in their mouths.

Eating an orange after a strawberry might not have been the best idea, since it's inherently more bitter. Reva's face scrunched up and did not return to its original shape until she swallowed.

"Okay," said Bob. "This should fix you." He handed her a pear and took one for himself. "The lofty pear is one of the sweetest fruits of all the field." He decided to flatter her. "Second only to you."

They finished their pears and, content, sat watching the workers in the fields nearby.

There were five fields across from the stream that were in various stages of production; rectangle arenas like giant ten-acre football fields filled with activity. On one, a large green tractor with small front wheels and giant back wheels towed an array of whirling discs that sliced into the ground, churning the earth and creating a dust cloud that swirled behind it.

On another field, small green dots filled the entire area while a sprinkler system on wheels slowly rolled on the edges, spraying firehose-worthy jets of water.

On a third field, the small green dots had grown to knee level and the only activity was the flirting butterflies that darted and floated above the leaves, sometimes disappearing, and then fluttering high in pairs, dancing in the wind.

And in yet another field, dozens of workers with wide--brimmed hats, long sleeve shirts and pants worked together in lines stretching across the field, leaving behind ruffled leaves as they harvested.

"It's great to see a working farm," said Bob. "Do you have these on your planet?"

"Yes."

"Well, are they something like this?"

"No, they are very different."

"How?"

"It's hard to explain. Let me show you."

"How are you going to show me, mind meld?"

"Your flat screen device. Is it powered up?"

Bob opened the notebook and with the single sound of a beep the screen lit up, showing a dark blue screen with small multi colored icons spread across the surface. He pushed it across the table until it was in front of her, and she turned the screen so that it was facing directly towards him.

"You wonder what I am doing, and how I'm going to show you our farming techniques," she said. "Our bodies are electric: yours, mine, every living thing carries a current of life. And if you want, you can focus your thoughts into that current, carrying them like the leaves you see on the stream below us, thoughts that can be transmitted directly into this device of yours."

He frowned, the corners of his mouth creasing while his eyes narrowed.

He was skeptical, she could sense it.

She smiled. "Watch." She placed her two forefingers on the upper corners of the back of the screen and closed her eyes.

The screen flickered and went dark, then images appeared. "This is a small farm on my planet."

It looked to be about the size of a football field.

On the screen was a large rectangle, a canopy steel frame covered with some type of black fabric sun block. There were lights evenly spaced across the field, misty water gently falling from sprinkler systems above, and below were row upon row of plastic-looking tubes, stretching across the field in perfect lines.

Growing in the middle of the tubes were green leafy plants, robust heads of what looked like lettuce. Each head of lettuce was growing snug in a separate plastic cup that was plugged into the long tubes.

A long deep steel trough stretching across the farm began to slide from one end to the other just above the lettuce. From the sides of the trough, mechanical robotic arms began to pluck the individual pots from the long plastic tubes and arrange them neatly inside. The harvesting went quickly, and when one row was completed, the trough with the mechanical arms moved ahead to the next tube.

Both ends of the tube that had just been harvested were opened with machines positioned on either side and water then poured out into a drainage swale. The machine on the near end inserted a ball of serrated blades on the end of a long metal snake. The snake began spinning as it entered the tube, cutting the remnant roots and pushing them out the other side, where they were collected by the opposite machine and piled onto a motorized sled.

The caps were re-installed, the water lines replaced. Another metal trough was next in line with tiny green plants in plastic pots. Robotic arms gently moved the pots from the trough to the tubes, plugging them snugly in place until each hole was filled. Then the trough moved onto the next tube that had been harvested and reamed clean.

Their perspective rose in the air and rotated until they could see hundreds of football field-sized rectangles stretching miles towards the towering spires of the city.

"It's a hydroponic farm," said Bob. "On a giant scale."

"We have no dust from our farming, it is all automated, from planting to harvesting. Plants grow faster in the water medium with growth fertilizer distributed according to need."

She pointed to the black canopy that was draped across the farm.

"Remember that we have a depleted ozone layer from the supernova gamma ray burst. The ultraviolet light from our sun is for the most part unfiltered, unimpeded and will burn any green plant. So, we block the sun with a woven fabric, the gentle lights are calibrated for optimal growing and are on all day and night."

She zoomed in on small glass lenses on the edges of the canopy, facing down.

"We have infrared optical cameras spaced evenly along the canopy that monitor the plants progress. The heat given off from the growth in their leaves is measured while computer systems determine what type and amount of fertilizer is needed for any given row of plants."

Bob was stunned. He got a sense that Reva was some type of engineer when she extricated their car from the hole outside Tahoe, but this was extraordinary.

"Where do you get your power? Combustion, solar?"

She smiled and shook her head. "We use solar for our spacecraft, of course, but on our planet we drill deep into the core and pump molten heat directly into vast arrays of turbines that generate electricity, so much that we can power our entire planet."

She zoomed out until they were hundreds of feet in the air. Now, they were looking down on hundreds of farms, a shiny metal grid miles and miles long and wide. They were connected by conveyor belts that were bringing the produce to a road and loaded into vehicles headed to the city far off in the distance. There was one steady line of vehicles loaded with produce, while another line of vehicles next to it came back empty.

"You're a race of engineers," Bob stated bluntly.

"We love to build machines, that is true. But with all of our ability, we couldn't build a machine to save our planet from the supernova."

"Now you have seen how our farms operate from planting to harvest. Of course there is more to it than this. Once the produce has been harvested, it's taken to a central warehouse where more machines collect the seeds to replant the fields anew."

"Since it's all automated, no one needs to work, is that right? No need to get your hands dirty?"

She smiled. "I should have said it is mostly automated, our world. Someone needs to design and build the machines, and we have machines for this also, but someone always needs to take care of the machines that take care of the machines, which is good for us as a society. We learned long ago that if a person doesn't work, doesn't have any task they need to accomplish, they..." Her words drifted off and she looked into the distance.

He prodded her shoulder with his index finger. "If people don't work, they what?"

She looked back at him with sad eyes. "They rot

from the inside. Just like that field that we just watched being harvested and mulched. Living, thinking beings are the same. We learned that lesson at a great price."

He waited for her to continue but she did not want to.

Then she shrugged her shoulders and winced. "It's kind of like the stories of your American Civil War that you showed me. The first cycle of years after we learned how to be fully automated were wonderful for most people. This was before the great awakening, when people were alone with their own thoughts and trapped in their own minds. The structure and fabric of people's relationships and ambitions faded into obscurity, no one needed to work or do anything throughout the long days and nights which stretched forever with no end in sight, a giant blur, just pick up their daily supply of food from the automatron and stare off into oblivion. Society slowly but surely deteriorated into anarchy. Bored and dulled into stupidity from a lack of ambition, a lack of the need to do anything more than lift your hand to your mouth with another morsel of food. A slow, evil spirit invaded the world, and it nearly burned all of society to the ground."

She was quiet again, looking off towards the shimmering heat rising from the road that ran off to the horizon. He could not sense anything from her, no emotion, no thoughts. All was empty.

And then she looked back at him.

"It was like a giant supernova exploded in the hearts and minds of the population, overwhelming everyone in its path, both innocent and oppressor, and when it was over and done, when nearly everyone on the planet was dead and buried, the few survivors that were left picked up the pieces and rebuilt what they could. It was like we were purged, like steel in a furnace, purifying us, hardening us. And then after the awakening, we all knew it could never happen to us again."

She took out a small plastic bag from the side pocket of her jacket. It was packed with old mulched leaves from the forest, blackened with age, from the fine bed that they shared in the mountain. She got up and walked over to a small bush struggling to survive in the dusty dry dirt, bent down, and poured the contents of the bag onto the ground. She got on her hands and knees, and with a small stick, began mixing it into the soil around the base of the trunk, singing a song as she worked. When she was satisfied with the result, she patted the soil around the little bush and kissed one of the leaves. Then, beaming from ear to ear, she came back and sat down next to him, held her palms towards him, and showed him her soiled hands, reddened from the dirt.

"Very nice," he said. "So people rot when they don't work eh?"

"We learned the hard way."

He winked at her and motioned with his thumb. "Maybe I could find a job right here, driving one of those tractors."

"I've seen how you drive, you would be good at that job."

He shook his head and frowned. "But I would get bored after a couple of days, driving down the same ruts, day after day after day. Having a job is one thing but having a job that you're uninterested with is almost as bad as not having a job at all. I need to figure out problems, devise solutions to mathematical equations, that's the kind of job that I enjoy."

"You should have fun at whatever you do."

"In fact, I have a mathematical problem right now I'd like to figure out. What do you think the odds are that two planets light years apart could produce two nearly identical species?"

She looked at him quizzically. "The odds?"

"Yeah, you know statistics, probability, likelihood, chance. It's like gambling, betting on something intangible, something about to happen, or not. What are the odds that we, you and I, are nearly identical, physically speaking. Apart from the fact that you are a female, and I am a male."

"What are the odds?" she asked again with a quizzical look on her face.

"That's the question."

"I would say one hundred percent."

He knew what she was going to say at the very instant that she said it. He'd heard about old married people that could read each other's minds and complete their partners sentences at will, but that was after living together for decades. And yet, here they were together for two days and it was like they'd been together for fifty years. Of course the odds were a hundred percent, after all, here they were. They were living, breathing proof. He gazed at the road as he drove and nodded. "Yeah, you're right."

Then a few moments later: "But what are the odds that there are any other planets with people like us?"

She smiled. "Also one hundred percent."

"How do you come to that conclusion?"

She laughed. "This time it's a guess. We called out to millions of stars and you're the only one that answered."

"Maybe I was just the only one that was listening."

There was a movement in the bushes near their table, and a small furry creature poked out its head looking at them with curious round eyes.

Reva's heart skipped a beat as she caught sight of its face, and Bob felt the sudden startled word in her mind.

Chalalabon.

The creature exited stealthily from the bush, first one careful paw then the other. Its sleek, silver-furred body extending from the round furry face and ears to the long tail pointing high in the air as it padded softly next to the bush.

He was like a regal king patrolling his private domain, an attitude of haughtiness on its face.

"Meow," it said.

"It's a cat," laughed Bob. He put his hand down

towards it and clicked his fingers together. "Here kitty-kitty." But the cat looked at him with disdain. In fact, thought Bob, it looked like it might be ready to attack. Suddenly, he remembered that he was afraid of cats, and he pulled his hand back. "It wants food. Sorry cat, we don't have anything you'd want."

"What does it want?" Reva asked.

It wants meat, and nothing else. I'll bet it would make mincemeat out of that creature on your planet that stalks you in the middle of the night."

She put out her hand like Bob, and clicked her fingers together just like he did, then whisper-sang: "Here kitty-kitty."

"Don't waste your time, look at that thing," Bob said, suddenly feeling stupid for calling to the cat first.

Its fur was dirty and ruffled and looked like it'd been sleeping in the mud down by the stream. There was mud on its paws.

"That looks like a wild cat," he said. "I'll bet it wouldn't come near you if you had fresh piece of tuna in your hand."

The cat looked at Reva with a steady gaze, and Bob could almost swear that he saw a mental connection occur. The cat's eyes wavered, the green reflective layer shimmered, while the slit-like black pupil narrowed as it watched Reva.

It took a careful step towards her with, stepping forward with one front paw, and then the other.

"Watch out that it doesn't scratch or bite you," warned Bob. "It might have rabies."

But Reva kept her eyes on the cat and began to sing a long sweet song, the song she sang to her Chalalabon in nights before, back up on the mountain by Tahoe.

The cat was entranced, looking at Reva unblinking eyes. It walked slowly towards Reva then closed its eyes and rubbed the side of its face against her outstretched hand.

"Well I'll be a monkey's uncle," said Bob, shaking his head. "There's no way in the world I thought that mangy cat would come anywhere near you. You know Reva, I do believe that the song you were singing is universal."

She reached out with her other hand, scooped up the cat and settled it onto her lap, curled it into a ball and held it gently while continuing to sing the song.

A few minutes went by as the song softened to a whisper, the cat put its face on its paws that were curled like little pillows on Reva's knees and fell asleep.

She looked over at Bob with a satisfied smile. "This isn't a Chalalabon, not exactly. It's longer and less furry, but it hears my song."

She looked down at it quizzically then brought her ear close. "It's making a funny sound."

Bob could hear it from where he was sitting. Like the sound of a small motor. "It's purring. It's what cats do when they're happy."

She looked back at Bob, and he knew what she was about to ask.

"Can we keep it?"

He scoffed and shook his head. The last thing they needed was another mouth to feed. Plus, how would they take it in the car? What if it decided to do it's 'business' on the back seat? What if while driving down the road the cat got irritated at something and jumped on the back of his neck and started biting and clawing him? It could be a disaster.

Bob shook his head with a definitive and absolute negative. "It probably belongs to somebody."

"But you said it was a wild cat. Doesn't that mean it lives in the wild on its own?"

He shook his head and pointed his finger at the sleeping fur. "I said it 'looks' like a wild cat. Maybe it's just having a bad hair day. Maybe it's taking a little vacation from that farmhouse way over there. Maybe it's a momma cat and has a liter of little kittens off in the bushes that need it. You wouldn't want to take it away from its family would you?"

Reva sighed.

"Don't worry," said Bob. "There's cats all over this planet. You can barely throw a rock into a bush without hitting one. Plus, maybe they converse in silent language among each other and once they get the word out that you have that Chalalabon song up your sleeve, they'll be clamoring to crawl up on your lap anywhere you go."

She sighed and glanced down at the sleeping furball with a look of love in her eyes and gently picked it up and set it on the ground.

The cat looked around grumpily, it's gentle repose abruptly disrupted.

"Run along now," said Reva sweetly to it. "Go back to your wild life."

Still it was confused and looked up at her with disappointment and betrayal.

Typical cat, thought Bob. He clapped his hands together loudly and the cat jumped in the air and bolted back into the bushes. They could hear the leaves rustling as it zigzagged through the undergrowth, back to the stream.

She turned to him, her cheeks were red. "You're mean."

"No, that's what you're supposed to do."

"Yes?"

"Of course. You had that poor cat, if you'll excuse my pun, in a catatonic state. The poor thing was hypnotized and lethargic. Heck, it could have been in a lot of danger in the condition it was in. Remember when it first showed up, how wary and alert it was? Ready to jump and run, or scratch and claw its way out of danger?"

"Well, yes…"

"That animal needs to ready to either fight or flee at a moment's notice. There's dogs and other cats and maybe even a mountain lion around that could ruin its day. That loud clap of mine snapped it out of the trance it was in and probably saved its life. Heck, that Chalalabon song almost put me to sleep."

He clapped his hands next to his ear and blinked

his eyes.

She smiled.

Soon, they got up from the table and walked back to the car.

15.

The road wound steadily down the mountain and the terrain changed from wooded and rocky to arid and rocky. The desert stretched out as far as the eyes could see while a thick brown haze obscured the horizon.

"There's an inversion in the atmosphere," he said. "And the desert is like a bowl holding all the goo together."

After half an hour she became sullen and sank back in the seat.

"What's the matter?" he asked. But he knew.

"It's hard to breath," she whispered.

"It's the atmosphere. The air pressure is higher, and the air is thicker, there's more of everything. The oxygen content is too high and it's overwhelming you."

"Yes."

He pulled onto the shoulder of the highway, got out his pad and looked at the map online.

They could either keep going forward or turn around and head back the way they'd come. Whichever way was quicker was the route they'd have to take, and quickly. He made the decision. Ten miles straight south at Sonora Junction, the road split in two: one heading east and then south towards Mono Lake, and other heading west and into the mountains towards the town of Dardanelle and the Stanislaus National Forest.

He pulled back onto the highway and floored it south. Ten minutes later they were at the junction. He turned right on the unmarked highway. A sign on the right shoulder read: 'STEEP GRADES AHEAD NOT ADVISABLE FOR TRUCKS OR TRAILERS'.

Perfect, thought Bob. Steep grades meant quick altitude. "Let's get some distance between us and sea level."

Rounded hills covered with brown grass and brush were in the immediate foreground ahead. Meanwhile, looming behind them were rough and craggy peaks, silent sentinels, and lonely foreboding mountains.

The road wound with a big sweeping half-mile long turn to the right and then another to the left, tires faintly screeching as the little blue car held the turns, and then a long straightaway up and towards a military facility.

The big shiny red sign mounted to the rock read: Marine Corps Mountain Warfare Training Center. The sign was set up next to an access road that was blocked off with giant boulders. Nearby, there was another square sign in black and white that read 'Road Closed'.

Now why, Bob thought, *would you have a nice entry sign and yet have the entry blocked off?*

Because there was another entry up ahead: he main gate with the guards and the machine guns. He slowed down a bit just in case there was a speed trap ahead, he didn't need to get pulled over again, especially not in front of a government facility on high alert.

Sure enough, as they rounded the corner, less than a mile away on the straightaway ahead was a large square entry. Up on the rise to the right, lining the plateau above them, was a red-roofed apartment, three stories high with sliding doors and porches, military housing. Next to that, long white buses, troop transports, and semi-trailers waited, full of equipment.

Bob slowed down under the speed limit, keeping both hands on the wheel and his eyes on the road ahead. They passed a square entrance big enough for a squadron of tanks, and in the corner of his eyes, Bob could see the gate house with the dark windows where the sentries could see out, but outsiders couldn't see in.

Then more buildings: square, steel-framed warehouses for weapons and equipment surrounded by barbed wire fencing. When he was well past the last building, watching it disappear in the rear-view mirror, he put the pedal to the metal and floored it again.

Reva looked pale, her head was resting against the side window. She needed altitude.

The nicely paved road became rough, with cracks running all the way across the road. Their tires thumped on the cracks every few seconds, while a sign on the side read: 'Road Closed in the Winter'.

Thank God it was summer. A large stream joined them on the left-hand side, parallel to the road. It was thirty feet wide, running fast over rounded boulders, turbulent white water tinged with green, remnant runoff from the snow melt last month. The driver side window was down, the sound of the rushing water filling the interior of the car.

The road slowly nudged upwards and Bob pressed down on the gas pedal to keep his speed up. Now they were climbing fast, the road getting rougher and steeper, trees obscuring the mountain peaks to the right and the left. The air was cooler up here.

They hit a steep grade, the sign on the right read: Elevation 2,000 feet. Reva began to stir in her seat and looked over at him, took a deep breath and exhaled slowly.

"I'm feeling better."

Bob nodded and kept up his speed. Soon, they were at three thousand feet, and then four, and when they hit another steep grade he slowed down a bit, not wanting to stress the car too much.

Five thousand feet. Reva stretched out her arms

and sighed.

"Thank you," she said.

It was a mad dash to get to this elevation and he decided to give the engine a rest, the temperature reading was a little high and the cylinders were beginning to knock, cheap gas and an overheated engine will do that every time. He found a level spot and pulled to the side, gravel crunching under the tires as they slowed to a stop.

Up ahead there were lonely mountain peaks on the right and left, magnificent grey and black granite citadels rose above the weathered hills beneath them, defiant to the elements of wind and rain, still growing in height as the tectonic plates, larger than the continents themselves, crashed into each other, raising them up to the heavens.

They got out the car and found a flat rock that had a good view, Reva stretching out on her back, enjoying the warmth of the sun-heated rock soak through her. She sighed and cradled her head in her folded hands. The rosy complexion had returned to her cheeks.

"That was a strange feeling. Everything was fine, I was enjoying being around one of your farms, and then my head started feeling dizzy, and it was hard to breathe. Now I feel fine, as though nothing ever happened."

"You had altitude sickness, but the opposite of what happens to us. Maybe you can adjust, but for now we'll stay above the five thousand-foot line, you seem to be okay now."

Bob pulled out his phone and switched it to a calculator as he factored the equations.

"Oxygen at sea level is, on average, twenty-point nine percent saturation. There's three quarters of one-point percent decrease on average per thousand foot of elevation. At five thousand feet we now have about eighteen percent less oxygen that at sea level, or about seventeen-point three percent saturation."

"I was feeling better at the two-thousand-foot mark, remember?"

"We're not taking any chances. Not yet anyways."

"Aren't I taking a chance just being here?"

He nodded. "True enough. We don't have to push the envelope though, do we?"

"You see those mountains?"

"Yes."

He switched his phone to map mode, studying it. "That peak on the right is Sonora Peak, altitude: eleven thousand four hundred and sixty feet. The one on the left is Leavitt Peak: eleven thousand five hundred and seventy-two feet. We have a winner. Can you believe it? Two giant mountains of granite, about five miles away from each other and there's only about a hundred feet of difference in height."

"They're like a family, growing up together."

He smiled at that. A family of mountains, one a little bigger than the other. Bragging rights at the dinner table.

"This family of mountains have a name you know.

The Sierra Nevada. From what I heard, they're getting bigger, somewhere around two inches a year."

He typed onto his phone, retrieving information.

"This mountain range is over four million years old, which is right about the time when humans split from apes, if what they say is true. These rocks have seen a lot of changes in this little world. This will be our home for a while." He gazed out at the serenity of the mountain range, the quiet strength of it. How small was one man, or all of mankind, next to it?

We could live here forever, he thought. With enough food and water and shelter over their heads, they wouldn't need anything else in the world. They could be homesteaders, cut down logs for a cabin, grow a giant garden. His mind drifted as he imagined the life they could lead, high up here in the mountains, unbridled by society and the pursuit of riches. All they needed was each other.

Her mood changed, he could sense it. He took his gaze from the mountains and looked down at her. The rosy complexion was draining away, her mouth slowly opening as a sort of dread shock entered her consciousness.

She sat up straight still holding her eyes closed, head down, breathing slowly, then looked at him with coal black eyes.

"It is happening," she said.

He could see the fear in her eyes and feel it in his mind.

"The second sentinel has perished."

He remembered what she told him. The second sentinel was positioned seven hundred million miles from their planet. The shock wave was travelling at ten percent the speed of light, sixty-seven million miles per hour. A freight train of death. It could travel that distance in ten hours, eleven hours at the most.

"We need your permission," she whispered.

Bob looked at his watch. Four-thirty in the afternoon and the shadows were deepening in the long crevasses on the southeastern flanks of the mountains that surrounded them.

Eleven hours from now, life would be wiped out on a planet six hundred and forty two light years away.

It would be three thirty in the morning pacific daylight time on the planet earth and there was nothing they could do to stop it.

It was strange to think of time and the finality of a moment fast approaching which could not be avoided or delayed.

A moment yet to come and they were tied to it with no escape.

A moment in time in which a planet full of vibrant life would cease to exist, instantaneously erased by a shock wave of radiated debris, and she was asking for permission to rescue them.

"Why do you need permission from me?"

"It is impossible without it."

"Why?"

"No one will come over without it. That's the way

it is with us, and no supernova or threat of extinction will ever change that. You know, and we know that none of us will ever be here forever anyways."

"But we're here now."

"Yes, we're all here now, and so we may as well do the right thing, and the right thing to do for us will never change. We need your permission, or they will all die."

"You're asking me to give the okay for an invasion."

"It's not an invasion if you're invited."

"You say that doing the right thing is the only way to go about it? Well I'm being honest by telling you right now that I can't speak for everyone on the planet. You're asking for permission that I can't give."

She hid her face in her hands filled with remorse.

Bob thought silently, he knew that she could hear him. *What's the worst that can happen? The complete annihilation of the human race for one thing. Reva's people come over to earth in the millions, across the vast distance of space, and it turns out they're not as pleasant and nice as advertised. Sure, just because Reva was calm and beautiful didn't mean they all were. What if the men were all devious cut-throats? The women all conniving backstabbing thieves? What if Reva was the only nice one of the whole bunch? As long as he had her in his life, why did he need the rest of them? Once they were here, whether they fit in or not maybe they could never get rid of them. The relatives from out of town that would never leave. This could all be a trick, a complicated ruse to get an invading army into the city, and Reva was their Trojan horse. A beautiful, loving present to an unsuspecting dupe.*

"Me," he said out loud.

It was beyond dangerous. Like looking into a bottomless pit, a wide gaping black hole and getting ready to blindly jump into it. Take a chance and there's no turning back, you and everyone else on the planet stuck with your decision for all of eternity. Or until you get wiped off the table like crumbs after a meal.

And then just as suddenly, Bob remembered the moment on the highway, the mote of dust, the brief connection with their creator as a semi-truck rambled by. The feeling in the back of his mind that they were not alone, they had never been alone, and that everything was going to be okay.

"I remember yesterday," he said. "You told me that everything was perfect on your world, and the supernova was sent to test you."

She nodded.

"Well, just maybe," he said. "It was sent to test us too. You have my permission. As a representative of the human race who is entrusted somehow to bestow this consent, since I was entrusted with bringing you here in the first place."

Reva uncovered her face and watched him, the slight beginning of relief washing over her.

"Besides," he said. "As one of our late great philosophers once said, and I quote: 'Sometimes it's better to ask for forgiveness than permission.'"

She threw her arms around him and hugged him tight. He could feel the warm tears welling up from her eyes on his cheek.

Time was running out.

"How many can you bring over?"

"Physically speaking we can bring over two each. It is draining as you know, and it takes time to recover. If we had all the time in the world, we could bring everyone over, but that's not the case, is it?"

He shook his head deep in thought. "We need to find a place that's out of the way, out of sight."

He put the tablet on his lap and looked at the satellite map. There was a gold icon showing where they were located parked next to the road. He zeroed in on Leavitt Peak, there was a large flat plateau just below it. He looked up from the tablet and pointed to it.

"That's our target, far enough off the road so we won't attract any attention."

Until the deed is done, he thought. *What happens then? How do you bring an alien population to a planet without attracting attention? Impossible. I'm looking at life in prison, or worse.* Fear crept into the back of his mind. *Don't think about that now*, he warned himself. *Just think about her.* He gazed over at Reva and shook his head as he marveled at her beauty.

"Let's get back in the car."

16.

They drove forward, higher into the mountain range. A sign on the side of the road read 'Sonora Pass, 9,624 ft.' and when they were parallel to Leavitt Peak, Bob spotted a side road. They pulled across the lane and onto the dirt road, around a corner, down across a dry creek bed and parked behind a bush on the other side.

Looming above them was the giant granite peak. He pulled out a backpack from the trunk and filled it with food, water bottles, a grey towel to use as a jacket, and as a last thought, the silk covering from the old man's hippy convention that he covered Reva with on their first night together. Only two nights ago and it seemed like forever.

Without a word, they started hiking up the granite mountain, the surface was hard and slick in places and they struggled to find the easy way up, grappling boulders and trees and whatever they could get their hands on for support. Within an hour they'd traveled a few hundred feet up in elevation and were on top of a sizeable plateau. The sun had set long ago behind the Sierra Nevada, and the color of the sky and their surroundings were a dull grey with the impending night shadows folding in around them.

"We can't go any farther," said Bob. "We might fall into a crack in the mountain, or step on a rattlesnake. This will have to do."

She nodded and they sat down to rest on the cold, hard mountain. They each took a small sip of water from the flask.

Night settled in, the blue edge of the horizon turning pitch black and stars lighting up the sky above and all around them. The fist-sized ball of stars in the constellation Pleiades was rising well above the Eastern horizon, followed by the V-shaped Taurus to the left of it, while below and to the right were the three evenly spaced stars of Orion's Belt angling down towards the horizon, above that the handle of the sword that held the red death star, Betelgeuse.

"What's your plan?" Bob asked.

"First I will bring over my brother, then my sister, and they will each bring over two others of their choosing, then each of them will bring over two of the next who are in line waiting, and on and on until our world comes to an end."

"Only two each?"

"That is the limit that one being can withstand in a short period of time after surviving the jump themselves."

"What about your Mom and your Dad?"

"They are too old and wouldn't survive the jump. You remember how you felt after you brought me over?"

"Sure I do. Like the wicked witch of the East from the Wizard of Oz."

"What?"

"The house fell on her."

"Oh."

He continued, "It was sort of what I imagine it would be like to be run over by a stampeding herd of buffalo, then finished off by a steamroller. The feeling you get when you take off on a jet airplane straight up into the sky and pop your ears, only your whole body both inside and out is your ear and the popping hurts like hell."

"That is the feeling," she said, "for the one who brings the jumper across. Multiply that feeling by a thousand for the one who jumps. The electrical current that runs through every nerve and synapse of your body is stretched to fit the one who jumps to you. We've studied this process for a millennium, and we still don't know exactly how it is accomplished. Most of it is through faith alone. Just believing it can be done is the engine that drives it. We don't know precisely how it is done, but one thing we know for certain, two jumps in one day is the limit. Three can kill you."

He was silent and even though he was stifling his thoughts she could feel his unease.

"Our people will travel to your world to live in peace, I promise you that, as long as you are certain that we have permission."

Even though the night was devoid of light he could see the stars shining on the surface of her black eyes as she looked at him.

"You don't need to ask twice."

"We need to be certain that we'll be welcome, for if not we might as well stay where we are and pass the test that was handed to us." Then she added. "And I will travel back to be with them until the end."

"There's no way I'm going to let that happen," he said.

Only time will tell, he thought to himself. *Who is ever truly welcome anywhere, outside of his own place that he calls home? A home carved out of the wilderness or out of a concrete nook and cranny of the largest city. Animals for the most part, and humans especially, are territorial. Survival at times meant having a space where you could block off everyone and everything else. The world can be a brutal place and it was usually safest to stay where you were. Stay with your friends and family. Stay with the people who were like you. Travel outside of your safe zone and you are risking everything. And yet sometimes that risk was the absolute key to survival. Not everyone could sit on top of a mountain peak and wait for food to be delivered to them.*

He knew that she was listening to his thoughts. She waited for him to finish. He went on, speaking out loud to soothe her.

"How could anyone prevent another from the pursuit of life, if in the course of that pursuit there was no threat. No living creature on this planet, or in the universe created so much as a grain of sand, a blade of grass, or a single molecule of the air that we breathe. We're all visitors, here at the mercy at the one who created all of this, from the stars at the farthest reaches of the universe, to the twinkle that I see in your eyes."

"No one has the right to prevent you from living here in peace with us, and if they think they do have that right, they are misguided. We all may be here now, but we're not going to be here forever, and even the place where we are headed, after this life, either good or bad, happy or sad, is nothing that we have made or can have any control over."

He took a deep breath. That was about as far reaching a diatribe as he could muster. In the deep recesses at the back of his mind, cold-hearted doubt was trying to come to the surface, and he stifled it before she could get a glimpse of it. Of course, something could go wrong, it always could. He threw a cold wet blanket of positive thought on the negative and smiled to thoroughly squash it. Everything was going to be okay.

"You'd better get started," he said.

17.

Ten thousand feet in elevation, freezing cold. Bob pulled the large grey towel out of his backpack and wrapped it around his shoulders, standing there shivering while Reva placed the colorful silk dress on her lap.

She sat on the hard ground with her elbows on her knees with her outstretched palms facing up, eyes closed tight, concentrating. Her breathing slowed and her body became still.

The minutes crawled by as Bob kept his eyes on her.

She seemed to tense up and the first one came across with a loud POP. Reva lost consciousness, slumping to the side but continued to hold onto the hands of the new comer, a young woman who looked nearly identical to herself.

She was completely naked with the same long black hair Reva had, a white mist rising off her reddish dark skin, dissipating into the night air.

Slowly, they both gained consciousness, began to breathe and looked over at each other, then the newcomer looked over at Bob with wonder.

"My sister," she said to Bob. The sister stood up and moved to the side, Reva quickly went into another trance, and a short time later there was another loud POP and what looked like a young man was suddenly there, and he slowly came to life, again looking around in wide-eyed wonder at his surroundings and up at Bob. His hair was also long and black, his eyes like coal.

Reva took longer to recover this time and remained slumped to the side. The young man continued to hold onto her hands until her eyelids fluttered, and she began to breathe again, small sips of breath, then a long deep inhale, her chest expanding, then rising slowly into a sitting position and looking at the one holding her hands.

"My brother," she said as her eyes focused, reaching her arms around him and holding him close, cheek against cheek. They both stood up together, and with their sister, formed a triangle hugging each other tight.

Reva stooped down to the silk dress that had fallen from her lap and helped her sister slide it over her head and smooth the edges over her shoulders and hips. Then she stepped over to Bob and, with a quick wordless grant of permission, took the towel from around his neck and helped her brother wrap it around his waist.

Then, Reva went back over to stand next to Bob as the brother and sister each bent over, picked up a large smooth stone and placed them carefully next to each other at the edge of the plateau. It was the same thing that Reva did when she transported to the hilltop in Tahoe just two days ago.

"We have to move fast now," said Reva to her siblings and they nodded in agreement, each of them picking a spot to the side, then sitting quietly with their hands held out palms up, eyes closed, barely breathing.

Two loud POPs and two more people appeared, slumped next to the siblings until they regained consciousness, then each of those newcomers found a smooth rock and placed them carefully next to where the siblings had placed theirs, then found a place further away and sat down holding their hands out.

Events were moving faster now as more and more dark-haired coal-eyed beings appeared, placed a rock in the growing pile, then moved to the sides and held out their hands.

Four POPs in succession, then ten, then twenty, then the sound did not stop and was a continuous POP, POP, POP, like a popcorn machine getting warmed up and gathering steam, the exploding sound spreading out across the mountain side, faster now like New Year's Eve in Chinatown, with hundreds of strings of firecrackers all going off at the same time, a gathering tumult as thousands and thousands of beings appeared and spread out to make room for more, and more. The mountainside turned alive with movement and sound, and still the popping went on, and on, increasing in volume and intensity on the ever-expanding edges.

Each being brought two friends across, and each of those brought another two, and on and on.

A hundred times a hundred times a hundred.

"Is a million," whispered Bob. "And a hundred times that is a hundred million." He began to have second thoughts, and a chill went up his spine. "My God what have I done? What if I've destroyed the human race?"

Remy, Reva's sister, sensed his anxiety, then reached out and held his hand.

"Don't worry Bob, everything will be okay."

She looked at him with her black, gentle eyes and he relaxed. That was his favorite saying. Everything was going to be okay.

Reva stayed by his side as the tumult increased, the loud sounds spreading out from them in every direction, and as it got farther and farther away the sound dimmed, but still it went on and on for hour after hour until the first light of dawn crept into the upper atmosphere and then suddenly the popping sound ceased, and was replaced by a steady sighing, moaning and soft crying. It filled the air around them.

"What's happened?" asked Bob. "Why are they crying?" He could barely make out the shapes of the thousands spread out around them.

"They are afraid, and they are also sad and mourning."

"Why has the popping stopped? Or has it gotten

so far away from us that we can't even hear it anymore. Is this all the people that are coming for now?"

She nodded, a fully human motion. "These are all that will ever come. They are mournful because our world has been destroyed, the shock wave from the super-nova has reached our atmosphere. Everyone that was left behind has been lost. The ones that are here now, are afraid for they are in a strange land, and don't know what their fate will be. We are at your mercy."

Now it was his turn to ease her anxiety as he squeezed her hand.

"Don't worry, we'll take care of your people. Sure there's a few bad apples, but humans for the most part are good and kind. We've been waiting a long time to find other life in the universe. And now you're here."

Tears began to flow from her eyes.

"Why do you weep?"

"I cry for my people, but I also cry for my Chalabon." She wiped the tears from her eyes, and yet they continued. "I cry for it all, the fire has destroyed the fields and all the unnamed beasts that reside throughout the planet, and all the creatures of the sea. It is all a wasteland, lifeless and silent. I cannot see it with my eyes, but I know that it is true. The end has come for our world."

18.

"Splendid," said Nicolas Gold as he shook the hand of the woman who had just introduced herself to him. Not many men could get away with saying the word 'splendid' without coming across as fake, conceited, or effeminate but Nick was able to consistently pull it off. It was his signature go-to greeting, especially with beautiful women.

His English accent resonated with a deep happy voice while his wide smile and jovial eyes projected a man who was completely at ease with his surroundings and his life.

Slightly heavy-set with curly brown hair, ruddy rounded cheeks and big thick hands, his friends had dubbed him a young Santa Claus, full of good humor and wisdom and ready to help a friend whenever needed.

With a Ph.D. in Biology and a minor in Molecular Thermodynamics, and a second Ph.D. in Mechanical Engineering with a minor in Space Systems Engineering, some people might say that he was an overblown overachiever, or someone who just liked the looks of a degree in a frame on the wall, but that was far from the case. He could care less about the accolades of the big letters next to his name. Nick loved being challenged with learning and mastering tough technical fields. Considering the extensive math and chemistry involved in the two arenas he chose to tackle, it was a challenge worthy of either someone of superhuman intellect, or as Nick would sometimes say during some of the darker days of the grueling ten years of study and testing: "I must be out of my mind, I should have been a simple farmer with my hands in the dirt, I would have been happier." Anyone who has been through quantum physics and thermodynamics will attest to that.

It was in that troubling time during college that Nick realized he was hopelessly stubborn in the pursuit of his goal. Nothing but total and complete victory would satisfy him. So, on and on he flailed, grinding through subject after subject, class after class, a relentless quest for perfection in an academic institution that rewarded no one with that satisfaction.

It was a humbling experience at times, failing classes because of his work load, pressing forward regardless of the constant worry and self-doubt; more than once it was two steps forward one step back. And yet somehow with a bullheaded determination and justified fear of failure, he'd break through with a sudden clarity and a great "AHA!" moment as the theoretical equations and lab experiments gelled within his cortex, an epiphany of sorts, and he felt as though exalted by the Gods.

He was working on his final project within the confines of the university, a dual thesis on biochemical quantum physics. He was researching space time and the physical changes in a human being traveling faster than the speed of light.

His mind was traveling faster than the speed of thought, and he finally graduated with honors. Some of the professors at the university were relieved to see him go since, by then, he could run circles around them.

Hired by NASA straight out of school, they flew him to the International Space Station for a one-month stint so he could expand on his molecular engineering thesis in zero gravity.

From there, he was on to designing interstellar spacecraft to accommodate human and other types of biological passengers. Then, the NSA came calling, they needed an expert to oversee a special department. It was a secret department that was placed out in the open, but no one really knew what its real purpose was.

As the head of the federal agency whose official purpose was supposed to be studying data but was in fact in charge of investigating and debunking UFO sightings, he needed a good sense of humor. For, after all, when one is dealing with crazy people, one needs to take it all with a grain of salt. Science: that was the key to the world, as far as he was concerned. He believed in cold hard facts, and nothing else. He based his entire life on the pursuit of the truth as far as aliens and UFO's were concerned.

His pursuit of the truth and penchant for skepticism began at a fairly early age. He was an only child with one parent, both mother and child abandoned one day by a husband and father who never returned.

Or so his mom said.

When he was around nine years old, he demanded that he and his mother acquire DNA testing since he, and his overactive imagination, needed to be convinced that she was in fact his mother and that he wasn't stolen at birth and raised under an assumed name. His mother rest her soul was very humble and agreed to what, at the time, was an expensive procedure.

The testing proved beyond a trillionth percentage point that they were in fact mother and son, and this solidified Nick's interest in the sciences.

Nothing in this entire world could be unexplained if you dug deep enough.

"Are you enjoying yourself?" the woman at his side bubbled with enthusiasm, hardly able to contain herself, her glittering evening gown with the low plunging neckline barely covering her cleavage.

"Absolutely," said Nick. "This party is the epitome of success. My congratulations, Madam."

She giggled. The chicks loved the accent, he'd found that out long ago when he first came to America as a college student from Oxford. The women loved it, but the guys, not so much. Especially when their girlfriends would follow him home from the classrooms and the bars, and so he had to ration the accent, and only use it when appropriate. This particular moment was an instant when he felt it absolutely appropriate to pour it on thick.

"I've always marveled at the astounding way that American women have of throwing superb social gatherings, or bashes, as we call them back home."

She giggled again, unable to say a word in reply, the bubbly in her system and the presence of the man next to her took the air right out of her.

"It's simply fabulous, this party of yours." Then he really dove into the accent and charming smile and repeated himself for good measure, drawing out the single word for maximum effect while looking deep in her eyes.

"Fabulous."

"I was always so interested in the space station and wondered if you could help me understand how it works."

"Certainly."

"For instance, since it's in a stationary orbit and the earth is pulling at it, why isn't there any gravity onboard, I mean they are always floating around, and it doesn't make sense to me since it's pulled down, or am I missing something?"

"Excellent question. You see the space station is not in a stationary orbit as you might think, it is actually falling towards the earth at about seventeen thousand five hundred miles per hour, however it is falling in a curve that exactly matches the curve of the earth, so that even though it's falling towards the horizon, it never reaches Earth. And since it is falling towards Earth the gravity is negated."

She made a pouty face and bit her lower lip. "I still don't understand."

The woman looked as if she was about to throw her arms around his neck when a man barged into the room, swirling a martini with an olive. A dirty martini, recognized Nicholas. The man was on the edge of being drunk, however, he was not yet slurring his words. He was still fairly steady on his feet and was obviously agitated at seeing Nicholas.

"Well, well so what do you know, here we have the stalwart defender of the known, and the unabashed attacker of all that is unknown and unseen. The unsullied lily white and shining pillar of the scientific community."

In Saint Nick's book this was the number one offense, not only interrupting a man's private conversation with a woman that was going rather nicely, but interrupting the conversation in a boorish manner. He must be dealt with accordingly, but in a manner that would not offend the young woman, since she was an innocent bystander, a civilian in an uncivil encounter. Luckily for her, this was one of the instances where a grain of salt came in handy, and Nicholas had a whole bag up his sleeve.

"Well, well, well," the man slurred again.

"Yes, you've said that already: referenced something that's deep and full of water," said Nick.

"The man jokes," said the drunk.

"Do I know you sir?" asked Nicholas politely, and yet unsmiling.

The drunk snorted and a bit of booze sloshed out of his martini glass and onto his shoe. "Do you know me?" And then a bit louder. "Do you *know* me?" Then, with a quieter conspiratorial voice he leaned in towards the couple. "Why, you made a fool out of me last year to all my friends and colleagues, so yes I do think you must in fact know me."

Nicholas frowned. "Can you elaborate? I don't recall ever meeting or speaking with you before. Maybe you have me confused with somebody else."

The man bowed. "Why yes knight of the round table of infinite knowledge and wisdom, let me refresh your memory. Late last year, while the International Space Station was over the Pacific Ocean, I was on-line monitoring the live feed when I noticed a cylindrical object suddenly appear in the distance. I studied it for a few minutes, and in my haste to be the first to announce its presence to the world, and gain fame and fortune, I announced that a presumed UFO, a potential alien space craft of some kind or other, had just materialized. Not a single hour went by before my nose was metaphorically rubbed in the dirt by you."

Nicholas held back the urge to smile, keeping a straight face with zero emotion. So, this was the quack who, with an internet bullhorn, blasted the video footage of the space debris.

It was time for Nicolas to gently put the drunk in his place and redirect his orbit so he could get back to schmoozing with the young lady.

"Kind sir let me explain that I meant no malice or ill will towards you or your discovery, I was only indicating that your observation was in error. I also wish to apologize and make it clear that I had no intention of categorizing you as a complete imbecile for pointing out to the entire world a piece of debris that originated from the space station itself and was not an alien spaceship."

"No ill will eh?"

"Why of course not. You, good sir, are merely a product of our own perfect evolution on this planet, nothing more or less. You must understand that one of our main human sensory systems, our sight, and what we see with our eyes, is functioning absolutely perfect for Earth conditions. But, we're still a local civilization on a specific planet. Moving beyond our globe-bound neighborhood tends to be visually confusing."

The beautiful woman tried to lighten the mood with a joke.

"I heard a funny story the other day…"

"Just a moment sweet one, I need to finish this point."

She looked at him disapprovingly, but he winked at her and continued.

"It's fascinating actually. Every astronaut is afflicted with it at some point in time no matter how much training takes place on terra firma to counteract it. You see, the human species, and all animals for that matter, who use sight as a means to navigate themselves. We all use points of reference in the back and foreground to orient ourselves. It's basic nature, is all done for the most part subconsciously, and is ingrained into our DNA. However, in space there is no immediate fore or background on which we can steady our sense of place, only empty space, and in the case of the space station the only point of reference is a rapidly advancing or receding globe, the Earth. You are either in pitch black space surrounded by a canopy of stars, or the steady unblinking full-blown light of our sun. When humans are walking about on the planet, while out in the sun, you will see shadows from objects on the ground or on other nearby objects, this also helps orient ourselves. Even if you are out and upon a featureless desert, or on the open ocean, you will at the very least see the shadow of your body, or the craft you are voyaging upon."

"On Earth, when an object large or small blocks sunlight from reaching another object, it casts a shadow on the other object's surface."

"Since the vacuum of space is void of any such surface, the space station's shadow, even though present, is unseen until suddenly it swallows up some debris or ice that is floating nearby, rendering that object invisible with the shadow. Then, it spits it back out as though it's emerging from a wormhole or appearing suddenly from some alien cloaking device."

"The camera on the space station is pointed back toward the receding horizon, and things will suddenly appear, as though they are coming up from behind the horizon, or behind a cloud."

"The object that you announced to the world was in fact a piece of metal the size of a can of soda that had separated from one of the retaining arms of the shuttle when it docked the week before, it was on a very slow elliptical orbit around the space station, taking days to circumnavigate it, and had on all the previous occasions been out of that particular camera's viewing plane. It came slowly out of the shadow of the space station, seemingly materializing out of thin air, and due to its proximity to the station and the abnormal distance for human perspective in comparison to Earth, it appeared to be a massive spacecraft that was about to invade our planet."

He wanted to add: 'Thank you for warning us of the impending doom,' but refrained from adding fuel to his fire.

"Yes, Dr. Know-it-all," slurred the drunk. "I realize that now. The sheer force of your rebuttal was uncalled for and has caused me irreparable damage to my reputation. I've lost work and quite of bit of funding as a result. I have you to thank for that."

"Money is overrated," said Nick. "Think of the panic you could have caused, people could have lost their lives running for the hills. I did you a favor by exposing the truth in as forceful a means to prevent disaster. I did you a courtesy, old man. If even a single person had lost their life or been injured because of your idiotic analysis of a camera phenomenon, you would have lost far more than your reputation, you could have lost every penny that you have, and been thrown in prison. You shouldn't be criticizing me, you should be thanking me."

The drunk man's face turned red with the final humiliation, and he drank the remainder of his martini with a single gulp and set the empty glass on a nearby table. "I'll thank you with a punch to the nose, how about that?"

He clenched both fists and raised them shoulder high in preparation for striking.

Nicholas, however, was a third degree black belt in both Karate and Jujitsu and though he carried a fair amount of confidence in his ability to withstand a physical attack, he was most concerned with making sure that no innocent bystanders were anywhere near an altercation.

He stepped quickly to the right to distance himself from the young lady and protect her from any wayward swinging fists, when towards the entrance of the ballroom a flurry of movement caught his eye.

Three tall men in crisp khaki uniforms had come through the double doors and were looking their way, following a finger being pointed, by one of the hosts of the party, straight at Nicholas. They moved quickly through the crowd and within seconds were at Nick's elbow.

The drunk had dropped his fists and was moved out of the way by the mere presence of three large men with guns on their belts. Two square jawed Marines and one older man with j silver tinged hair above his earlobes. They were polite and yet firm in appearance and it was obvious that a person would do well to get along with them.

"Nicholas Gold?" asked the older one.

"That's me," said Nick grimly. "Why the guns? Are you here to arrest me?"

"We're here to protect you."

"From what? I could have handled this drunk buffoon."

The older man looked sternly at the wobbly drunk and back to Nick. He made no comment on the obvious confrontation.

"We need you to come with us, sir." Then he leaned in to speak softly to Nick so no one else could hear what was said. "This is a matter of national urgency. General Stanton needs to see you right away. We have a helicopter transport at an empty field one mile from here."

"Stanton?"

Marine Corps General 'Bullnose' Stanton made his mark in a couple of conflicts in the Middle East. One in particular when he was on a reconnaissance mission flying near a battle zone. He'd just been promoted to a one star General and as such, was a prime target for the enemy. Protocol was for him to be in a secure bomb-proof command shelter but that wasn't his style. He was in one of three Apache helicopters observing the perimeter of the battle when they got word of a platoon nearby that was in trouble. He ordered the helicopters to attack immediately. The captain of the chopper insisted that they drop off the General first but 'ol Bullnose overrode him and in they went. He was a no-nonsense commander, more concerned with the well-being of his troops than himself.

When he shouted for you to fall in line front and center, you didn't say no.

Nick sighed with resignation, reached out for the young woman's hand, gently kissed it, and followed the Marines towards the door.

19.

The helicopter landed in a semi-circle clearing. Two heavily armed Marines were at the door in a split second to assist him out onto terra firma, each with a firm hand on his elbows as he found his footing. He held onto his hat in the rotor wash as the chopper idled.

"This way sir!" barked the one on his right as they scampered away from the clearing.

When they had travelled about a hundred feet, the shrill whine of the turbine engines increased quickly, the main rotor blades thumped loudly, and the helicopter lifted up into the air. Nick turned to watch as the craft hovered fifty feet off the ground, rotated one hundred and eighty degrees away from them, tilted its nose cone down, and roared off into the sky, seemingly hell-bent on another mission.

Somewhere in the distance but out of sight, hidden by rocks and valleys, he could hear trucks running and commands being yelled.

One of the Marines still had his hand on Nick's elbow and he turned to him, prying the fingers away.

"I've got this, okay? I can walk on my own without your assistance."

The Marine's face didn't break but Nick could sense a palpable fear beneath the steady exterior. Pre-combat anxiety.

The soldier insisted. "We have orders to deliver you on the double, sir."

"Well point to where we are heading and get out of my way then."

The Marine motioned with his hand then bolted forward to lead the way, and off they went.

They were heading for a group of green field tents. They were ten-foot high, fifteen-foot wide, fifty-footlong and intersected at the middle like half buried giant green worms with flexible ribs. Nick recognized them as portable quick set-up medical and command posts used in war zones and disaster areas. They could be dropped by a helicopter, unpacked and be fully operational in five minutes.

Some of the green pods were a different shape and a slightly different shade of green, with thicker walls and higher roofs. They were a new generation of quarantine field tent, the kind the government procured for the Ebola disasters in Africa. They were hermetically sealed with generators and air scrubbers on the exterior, with long white flexible tubes funneling the good air in, and red tubes pulling the bad air out. The air scrubber was the size of a large refrigerator laying on its side with layers of filters soaked in bleach and, in one chamber, a mini blast furnace burned the air before exiting. There were also full body wash stations, incinerators for clothes, double locked entries.

Ebola couldn't be cured, so the method of preventing an outbreak was complete and total quarantine, including the air that was being exhaled from the victims.

Some people speculated that the Ebola outbreak was orchestrated by the government for the explicit purpose to test equipment and methods of control for something really bad. Something worse than Ebola, some future unknown biological event that would need to be contained, and quickly.

One of Nick's conspiracy friends asked him to look into it, but he couldn't find anything to substantiate a government plot. The outbreak was genuine, and terrible. And it was just what was needed to practice containment. Though, he'd never think for a minute that the government would pass up a chance to get a leg up on the competition when a disaster happened.

They headed for the entrance that was guarded by two more Marines, young grim-faced grunts, holding their assault rifles at the ready, fingers on the trigger,

Nick could see that the safeties were off. Neither one of them smiled nor gave recognition to the visitors, their eyes stayed on the perimeter, watching for any potential danger.

They looked combat-ready, with an edge of anxiety. The lead Marine opened the door for Nick, and he walked in. The light inside was red like the interior of a conning tower on a submarine right before surfacing at night when submariners needed to be able to see. Two more Marines were guarding the inside of the door facing each other on opposite sides of the entryway. They gazed menacingly at all four of the new visitors and stepped aside to let them pass. They walked into a bustling bee hive of activity towards a desk with a man behind it. The man wore a brown khaki shirt and tie with the sleeves rolled up past his elbows and four stars on his collar. He was watching a monitor when he noticed the activity in his peripheral vision and looked up to see Nick and his armed guards approaching. He nodded, reached out, and shook Nick's hand.

"Thanks for coming."

"I didn't think I had a choice."

"You didn't, and believe me, you wouldn't miss this for the world. What do you know so far?"

"Nothing."

"Good. We have tight wraps on this situation, and we're gonna keep it that way. Come with me." He grabbed two pairs of field binoculars and held one out towards Nick.

"You ever use one of these before?"

Nick turned them in his hands, sure he'd used them before, but not this type. "Night vision field glasses."

"Correct. These two buttons on top here increase and decrease the magnification. They're set to the lowest mag now. Let's go."

They walked to the back end of the tent past two guards, and out into the night. The stars were shining bright as they walked to the edge of a gully. They were on a plateau; the back end of the command tent was tight to the edge of a cliff. The general pointed.

"Down there."

It took Nick a moment to lift the large binoculars and set them to his eyes, the cushions on the eyepieces forming a tight bond to his eye sockets. He scanned the valley floor.

"What am I looking for?"

The general reached over and gently guided the front of the binoculars down and to the right, and then Nick saw a huddled mass of something, a blob of round shapes.

"Pick a spot and steady your hands, then increase the magnification with that button."

The blob got smaller and the round shapes got bigger, hundreds now. Nick increased the magnification in increments until there were just a few round shapes, and then just one. It filled the frame of the lens. The image was grainy and jumped with his unsteady hands, but it was most definitely the shape of a head with eyes and ears and long black hair, and the body beneath the head was nude.

Keeping the magnification the same he slowly scanned the crowd. They all looked nearly identical in size and shape, all nude, and huddling together shoulder to shoulder front to back, side to side sitting wedged together in a giant breathing mass. Thousands upon thousands of living tissue.

A creeping tingle of dread crept down his neck. "What is this?" Nick whispered.

"We don't know yet," said the general. "That's why you're here."

Nick pulled back the magnification until it was at its lowest again, and the whole mass of beings fit into and filled the frame of his vision. Then, he scanned the edges until he saw other shapes far away from the mass. They were scattered around the edges every hundred feet and at least a football field away from the mass. He zeroed in on one of the shapes and saw a uniformed man crouching with an assault rifle aimed at the pack and ready.

"You have them surrounded like a herd of animals. Did you crowd them into a group? Is this some kind of test? A crowd control experiment?"

"We didn't do anything, we found them like this."

"Explain please."

"At around o-three hundred hours this morning and just before dawn, the Marine Mountain Training Center at the base of this mountain noticed a spike in sound vibrations coming from our sensors in one of our training zones just to the north of this area. We had a platoon deployed on an exercise and we sent them to investigate. They came upon this group huddled together just as you see them now. They called base, who sent up a helicopter reconnaissance flight, and they in turn called command, who called me. I gave the order to cordon off this entire area and blackout all communication coming in and out of this arena. We have imaging software as you know that can count how many beans are in a coffee field, how many stars are in a galaxy, or how many heads are on a battlefield."

"Yes, I helped develop it."

"I'm aware of that, you should be confident of the accuracy. There are one hundred and twenty-seven thousand five hundred and fifty-one heads in that small area. Did you notice the round shape of that gathering?"

"Yes."

"Over a hundred thousand beings crowded neatly into a perfectly round shape. Equidistant from side to side, top to bottom. We're seven miles from the nearest road in some of the most rugged country in the Sierra Nevada mountain range. That is why we have a training facility here. To find a single person here is unusual, and those that do venture here are well equipped. To find a crowd this size, none of them with clothing suddenly appear seemingly out of nowhere set off a big alarm. I don't like alarms."

"What is this, some kind of elaborate hoax?"

"We don't know what it is."

"Maybe someone set up a hundred thousand mannequins and placed a couple of real people with wigs in the middle and on the edges to make it look like they're all real. Kind of like a crop circle with people. These idiots will try anything to get attention. There's probably secret cameras set up all over the place recording our every move to make us look stupid."

"We thought of that."

"You think they're all real?"

"They're not mannequins. We did an infrared scan. They all have a heat signature."

Nick looked through the binoculars again, filling the frame with the whole giant round group, and then increased the magnification till he could make out a single face. It looked like a young man, long dark hair, dark eyes, smooth olive skin, calm demeanor, eyes open, every now and then blinking, looking straight ahead, nostrils flaring slightly as though breathing softly through them. Nick panned right then left and into the center of the group, observing young men and women with much of the same features: long dark hair, dark eyes, olive skin, all with wide eyes, and all facing out from the center. And yet, when Nick looked towards the center of the gathering there was no specific individual. They were all facing outward from the center in all directions, like a giant, living wheel.

"What do you think?" asked the general.

"What do I think?" Nick paused. "I think it looks like a colony of Myxococcus xanthus bacteria spores. They're a perfectly round bacterium that exist in the soil and feeds on other species of bacteria. It's usually found in single-species clusters, called swarms, which act as a collective unit and show coordinated movement in response to environmental cues. The bacteria are also able to segregate to form sedentary spores that are impervious to dehydration. They can lie dormant for years and come back to life with a single drop of rain. That's what I think. What I actually know, however, is that I don't know for certain what it is. On first glance I don't think it's human, even though the faces look so. How could you ever get that many people to cooperate to remain still and perfectly arranged in such a manner? It's not in our DNA. Maybe they're robots. I'm still clinging to the elaborate hoax theory. How long ago did you find them?"

"About ten hours ago."

"And have they moved?"

"Not an inch."

"And how did you find them again?"

"Our sensors mounted in this area detected unusual sounds."

"Shuffling feet? Coughing? Laughing and talking, can you elaborate?"

"Popping."

"Popping?"

"Like the sound of a giant kettle of popcorn that went on for an hour and then was silent."

Nick was quiet as his mind digested what he was looking at and what he had just heard.

"I need to go down there and see them."

"There's no need for that."

"Why?"

"We have one here."

"Only one?"

"For now that's all we needed. It's a female. We also have a male, who says he's human."

"He says he's human? So he can talk." The skeptic in Nick was rising to the surface, and he stifled a laugh, this was not the time for mocking. "What does she say?"

The general was stoic. "She says she's from another planet, and they are all asking for permission to stay."

Nick narrowed his eyes. "She speaks?"

"Perfect English."

Nick could contain himself no longer and chuckled. "Oh this is one for the books. What is this, an elaborate prank? Is someone setting me up?"

"I was hoping you'd say that," said the general. I need a cynic right now."

"Why?"

"Because I'm not one, and I need to find out what is going on here before any of these things escape."

Things.

"I'll tell you something else," said the General. "No one gets off this mountain until we find out what's going on. A hundred thousand people don't just show up without an explanation."

Nick pressed his hands together in the gesture of a prayer. "Lead the way sir."

20.

They travelled down another half-round green corridor to yet another door guarded again by two heavily armed Marines. Rifles at the ready, eyes steady. They did not salute the general or even acknowledge his presence but focused all their attention on Nick presumably to make sure he wasn't holding the general hostage and using him to bust out their prisoners. The one on the right reached over and looked through the small window on the door, knocked twice, then once again, and opened it slowly.

The two Marines on the other side faced the interior of the room and were watching a plexiglass wall that was connected to this room by a smaller tube, sealed on both ends.

"It's a quarantine chamber," stated Nick matter-of-factly.

"Indeed," said the general. "After you," he continued.

They went into a room adjacent to the quarantine

chamber. There was a long desk with stacks of papers and charts, and an x-ray viewer box lit up with two shiny black negatives, one an image of an entire body, and another a close-up of a brain. A man wearing a long white lab coat was standing in the center of the room and he shook hands with Nick. Embroidered on the coat were the words: 'Captain Marcus O'Neil, MD.' There was a large rectangular window on the wall in between the rooms, and Nick walked up and put his face an inch away from it to studied the people inside. They did not acknowledge him or even seem to notice him.

"One-way mirror?"

"Yes."

A man and a woman were seated on separate chairs next to each other in the far-right corner of the room. Their demeanor was calm, which struck Nick as quite unusual given the circumstances. The woman was exotic and beautiful, and Nick found himself instantly attracted to her sleek looks. Long dark hair, dark eyes, perfect round facial features, dark olive skin.

Her facial expression bordered on a hopeful amusement, as though she was just told a funny joke and was waiting for the punchline.

The man, however, was a bit ruffled on the edges, hair crumpled, with a look of quiet anxiety in his eyes, like a man resigned to his fate, standing at the foot of the gallows before the bell tower signaled the time for his execution.

What struck Nick is that, at the instant, he felt an

attraction to the woman. She seemed to look directly at him, although that could not be possible with the mirrored window. He shook it off as coincidence.

"Why these two?" he asked.

The general came and stood next to him and looked through the window. "They were standing about a hundred yards from the main group when our crew got here. They seemed to be waiting for us, and indeed when our point man came into contact, they asked to speak with someone in charge. Said they needed permission."

Nick was fascinated with the woman, and could barely take his eyes off of her, she was incredibly beautiful. Reluctantly he tore his gaze away and walked over to the table.

"Your medical crew did some tests?" Nick asked the man in the white coat.

"Blood analysis, mouth swabs, DNA, ultrasound, x-rays, eye exams.

"What do you think," asked Nick.

"I don't know yet," said the doctor. "Take a look."

Nick sat down and started reading the charts. He separated the piles to opposite sides of the desk and started with the mans.

At the top of the charts was a single name in bold letters: BOB.

The blood work numbers were normal and within range of a healthy twenty-eight-year-old man. Blood type AB, typical for a Caucasian man. His blood pressure and heartbeat were a little elevated but that would come from being in captivity with armed guards.

X-rays were normal, the small bone in the bottom half of his leg, his fibula must have been broken at some time in his life and there was the tell-tale dark line of a fracture that had healed and a small metal plate, that is most likely titanium, still attached. The DNA was normal. Eye exam, normal.

Nick turned to the woman's file.

REVA.

The blood work also looked mostly normal for a female in her late twenties. Mostly normal except for the blood type. It was indeterminable, somewhere in between A, and ABO. The white blood cells were a little on the low side, there was a marked decrease in the hemoglobin phenotype, the red blood cell that carries oxygen. The woman's blood type and structure resemble that of a lifelong Tibetan who lived at an elevation over fourteen thousand feet.

The DNA also looks, for the most part, normal for a mixture of Caucasian and Asian ancestry, but there was one anomaly that stuck out.

"What's this?" whispered Nick as he looked closer at the DNA analysis, and he whistled softly at one of the lines. He'd seen this before. "It looks like a high-altitude variant of the EPAS1 gene." This was the gene that was stimulated when oxygen levels in the blood dropped, triggering an increased production of hemoglobin. "It's the Denisovan gene." Named after the prehistoric hominids that went extinct forty-five thousand years ago. Modern day Tibetans inherited a small percentage of the super gene when their ancestors interbred with the Denisovans on their way through the upper altitude regions of China.

He turned to the X-rays and clipped two films on the light box. Body structure normal. Brain structure, normal except for a small extra bump in the cerebral cortex region, the area responsible for dreams.

Eye exam, and this is where the red flag started waving in front of Nick. Her eyeballs were larger than normal in size, the cornea more rounded, the white of the eye called the Sclera was a grey black, the iris and the pupil both dark black in color, the iris itself very slow in contracting when a light was shined directly at it, and it retained a pinprick of an opening long after the light was removed. This was the type of eye that would be well suited to a bright location like the white sand desert, or a snow field with the sun shining directly on it.

"There's something else," said the Doctor. "Take a closer look at the blood analysis."

Nick scrolled through the numbers. "She's pregnant."

"The ultrasound was negative, so it must be a recent event."

"Fascinating," said Nick. He looked up at the General. "Mind if I go inside and have a chat?"

21.

The pneumatic door closed behind him with a hiss as the airlock was re-secured. He held a yellow legal pad and pen in one hand. The other he held out in an open palm gesture of greeting.

"Hello," said Nick. "My name is Nicholas Gold and I'm here to ask you a few questions. This isn't a formal affair, we can just have a little conversation if that's okay?"

The ruffled man nodded. "I'm Bob, and this is Reva."

She smiled.

"Splendid," said Nick. "Thank you." He strolled past the mirrored wall and pulled up a chair that was in the opposite corner from the prisoners. "Well, this is nice," he said as he settled into the chair. "Do you know why I'm here?"

"To ask us some questions," said Bob. "As you just told us."

"There's a man in the next room on the other side of that mirror who is the general of a large army, and he told me that the young lady here is from another planet. I'll be blunt with you. I don't believe anything of the sort. I'm what you might call the chief skeptic."

Bob looked over at Reva, and she was looking straight at Nick.

Do I have your permission to speak with you? she asked, and yet it wasn't with her lips. They were closed, and yet Nick clearly heard her. It wasn't a voice in his ears, and yet it was a voice that resonated from the front, all the way to the rear lobes of his mind. His eyes widened slightly, while the hackles on the back of his neck stood erect as a light tingle went down his spine.

He was stunned to silence, un-moving, un-deciding, shocked by what he was experiencing. He could see Bob looking at him from the corner of his eyes. Bob knew what was happening and he was nodding his head slowly. He knew.

The air in the room grew thick with silence, and the walls seemed to close in on them.

Can I speak with you? she asked again without speaking. *Do I have your permission, sir?*

Yes, Nick answered back without moving his lips, only thinking it. The sound of the thought reverberated in the center of his voice box but did not exit, it was both infuriating and exhilarating, as though he was an animal trapped in a box, unspeaking and yet speaking. *Yes*, he thought again, the hairs now standing on his arms, suddenly anxious and afraid.

She was in his mind. Talking to him. Nick's face slackened as he realized what was happening. This was real.

Bob gave us permission, she thought towards him. *We come in harmony. Your planet has saved us, and we are forever grateful. We come to you in peace. Two by two we come, each two brings another two, and so on and so on. Seventeen rounds of two by two and we are done, we are complete, this is all that will come here forever and ever. Our world, our planet is destroyed, and we are all that is left.*

Nick looked down at the legal pad on his knee and wrote down the number. Seventeen rounds of two. Each two brings two. That is two to the seventeenth power. He wrote quickly. Two to the seventeenth power equals one hundred thirty-one thousand and seventy two, and he distinctly remembered the general saying that the software program counted exactly one hundred thirty one thousand and seventy. There were two missing. He thought the question to Reva.

You brought the first two, and they each brought two for seventeen rounds?

Yes.

We're missing two.

Not missing,

What?

It is our custom, from the days before all remembering. Whenever our tribe, our people travel to a new land, we always send two, one male one female to a separate location to wait, in reserve in case disaster strikes the rest of us.

A strange foreboding was rising in Nick, and the thought that he was thinking was pure and wishful in nature and yet rose out of him like a bubble from a swamp. He asked, *Whenever you travel to a new land on your old planet?*

Her face was stoic. *Any new land.*

This isn't the first time you've traveled between planets, is it?

How could we possibly know where we came from? Do you?

No, thought Nick. It was a question he'd struggled with all his life. *As far back as I can remember, it's as though I just showed up, I'm here, I'm alive, I'm thinking and reacting and breathing and wondering, and yet I can't really explain it, even with the most extensive cold hard science. I'm here and there's really no explanation for it, this is something I've known for a long time. Everyone alive on this planet today is here and I can guarantee you that not one of them has a completely definitive explanation why.*

He could hear her voice in his head clearly: *Isn't the fact that we are here explanation enough?*

It should be, however, an inquisitive mind will ask why. It doesn't matter the situation, there's always going to be the nagging question at the back of that inquisitive mind. Why? Now I have a question for you. The people who brought me here did so for a specific reason, to find out if you are in fact an alien. There's a lot of tricks that can be played to make a single person, or an entire population, believe anything. Mass hypnosis is not a new invention. For the sake of simplicity, I'll simply ask you. Are you an alien?

She smiled. *Do you believe that this world exists?*

He cocked his head to the side. *Is this a trick?*

She continued. *Do you think there's a possibility that you could be a figment of your own imagination?*

I see where you're going with this. Of course I believe that this world exists and I do believe that I exist within the framework of this world I don't believe that this world and everything in it is a physical manifest of my imagination. I'm alive, I'm breathing, I'm thinking, I'm existing. For now, anyways.

She smiled again, *Yes, for now. But you haven't always been here have you?*

He shook his head. *No one has been here forever. And no one will be here forever.*

Her smile faded and was replaced with remorse. *But we're here now. You believe that.*

Yes, we're here now. "And how did we arrive in the here and now. Perhaps we're the figment of someone else's imagination?

He focused, making sure his thoughts would go to her clearly. *We're a biological byproduct of billions of years of evolution, the building blocks of atoms and elements and molecules joining and binding in a primordial soup, climbing out of the swamp. Yes. We're the byproduct of everything that makes up this universe, every chemical and atomic energy that exists throughout the farthest reaches of the cosmos and on this planet. We are not an oasis, as some would say. There's life spread from one end of the universe to the other, of that I'm completely assured, but I do not believe that the vast distances and restrictions on biological existence make it even remotely possible to travel between the stars, and I have made it my life's work to repudiate any attempt to validate the presence of aliens on our planet.*

You believe that the building blocks of life exist throughout the universe?

Yes, he admitted.

And so it's possible that life exactly as exists on this planet could exist on another planet somewhere in the universe.

Of course.

And if that life is made of the same atoms and elements and molecules that are found throughout the universe and that life form suddenly arrived on your planet, why would you ask if it was an alien?

Of this planet, he corrected.

We think alike, you and I, she thought, still communicating with him. *We are all part of this universe, the byproducts of all the material that makes it. And yet I know that we did not make the material. Not one single atom, or element, or combination of atoms did you or I devise and combine to produce this world and everything in it. We are somehow just here, and there is a higher power that is responsible. We are all part of this universe, for now anyways, and when our biological bodies are spent, we'll all go back into that primordial soup, as you say.*

Yes.

We don't own this world, but we will forever be a part of it.

Yes, in one form or another we'll always be part of this world, this universe, even when all time is spent and the stars collapse back onto themselves and explode into a new big bang, we'll be part and parcel of the entire spark.

Then how can you ask me if I'm an alien?

Because it isn't possible.

You need proof.

It's more than a need with me. It's a necessity. I live and breathe in the certainty of what I know to be true, and nothing less. Without pure definitive proof I will not believe in anything.

There is no pure definitive proof that I can give to you then.

This mind reading, he thought, this *conversation that we are having now could be explained, somehow, I just don't know how at this point in time. I'll admit it's interesting, but there have been times in the past where people have been hypnotized into believing almost anything.*

You'll never believe.

You say that you're able to transport from one place to the next, he thought, *and that you transported from another planet many light years away.*

You are looking at proof of that.

But no one witnessed the event.

Bob did.

Nick looked over at Bob who nodded and said out loud. "I did witness it." When Bob saw the surprise on Nick's face he continued. "And yes, I can hear your conversation even though you are not speaking out loud."

"I thought I had to give you permission."

"Reva has already given me hers, and your thoughts resonate through her to me."

"This is insane," said Nick out loud, and he sat quiet in thought for a moment before turning back to Reva. "If you can transport yourself through time and space from one planet to the next, then surely you can transport from one end of this room to the next. We have cameras and we'll film it, to prove, or disprove it. Will you agree to that?"

"Of course," said Reva out loud.

"No! "shouted Bob, and they both looked at him in surprise. "She can't. Not now, not tonight."

"Just what I thought," said Nick.

"She can't because it's too soon after transporting her family."

"What in blazes are you talking about?"

"Two is their limit for a day, and it has been less than a day since Reva brought the first two over. Another one this quickly could kill her."

"You're stalling for time."

"It's true," said Reva. "I could die from the exertion. But if it would save my family, my people, it would be worth it to me. But you still wouldn't believe, would you?"

Nick studied her carefully while she continued.

"Even if you saw me with your own eyes disappear from one place, and then reappear in another you would not believe it actually happened. Even if you filmed it and watched in slow motion over and over again you would not believe. You would spend your entire life trying to explain it away."

"You're probably right, but it doesn't matter does it? You would never be able to pull it off anyways. This is an elaborate hoax of some sort."

Reva persisted. "You wouldn't believe it, any of this, unless you yourself experience it."

Bob looked over at her and slumped back in his chair, as he realized the inevitable.

"With your permission I will transport you from one end of this room to the other. Film it all you want from every corner and every angle, in black and white or color, slow motion, infrared, x-ray, or any other film medium or recording device for your detailed analysis and study. None of that will matter since it cannot be studied or analyzed. You will never believe what you can only see with your eyes. However, when your entire being is transported through time and space, stretched and pulled and dispersed from one place to another you will know without a doubt that what we say is true. For to transport is to be awakened."

Nick looked over at the mirrored wall. More uncertainty was seeping through his ironclad wall of skepticism.

The mind reading was strange and unusual, and yet had always seemed a possibility.

Extensive studies had been done, Nick himself had participated in double blind experiments where people were shown objects in one room and a mind reader would attempt to guess what they were looking at.

For the most part, ninety-nine-point nine percent of the time they were wrong. But every now and then an anomaly would appear when they least expected it.

Usually it happened when the scientists let their guard down, experiments were tedious and laborious, and put you into a mundane trance, and that is when the subjects would seem to get more of the answers correct. As though by letting go of one's ego, the mind was more receptive to outside influences, thought waves and suggestions.

Nick was afraid that exact thing was happening to him at this very moment, during the whole parade of getting dragged out of the party by a squad of gun-toting military men, the medical tents, the binoculars and the crowd of naked men and women in the middle of the wilderness on top of a mountain.

Or, maybe someone slipped a drug into my drink at the party, and I'm hallucinating all or most of this, he thought.

"Alright," said Nick out loud. "Go ahead and transport me. But not from one side of this room to the other, that would be too easy to fake. From well outside this room, outside this tent in fact. Outside of any eye contact between us."

"Reva…" muttered Bob as a worried look crossed his face.

"It'll be alright Bob," she soothed, turning towards him and touching the top of his hand with hers.

Her fingers lingered on top of his for a moment, kind thoughts passing between each other, and then she turned back to Nick with her black eyes and spoke to him with her voice so that the watchers behind the window could hear her. "Go wherever you want, kind sir, as far away as you need to give yourself comfort. The quieter the location, the less distraction, the better. Calm yourself, calm your mind and fill your heart with goodness and light. Free yourself from any anxiety or fear. When you are ready just reach out to me with your mind, search for me with all your might, and I will bring you to me."

Nick looked towards the mirrored window and nodded then walked towards the exit door, standing in front of it until he heard the click of the lock opening.

He walked in, closed the door behind him and heard the gaskets at the door frame swell into place, blocking any air from exiting. He then took off all his clothes and placed them in the stainless-steel incinerator, closing the lid with a click, and pressed the button. With a muffled whoosh the clothes were burned to a crisp. He held his hands over his head and closed his eyes as the nozzles above him and to the sides sprayed the antimicrobial foam on every inch of his body.

When the spray was complete, he had to feel with his hands, keeping his eyes closed, pushing against the next door and into the adjacent room. Behind him again the door frame gaskets hissed into placed and more jets sprayed him from every side, but this time it was pure water and when that was done, he wiped his eyelids clean with the tips of his fingers and pushed the door to the final room.

Gaskets hissing into place, he found the towel, dried off then re-dressed into a new jumpsuit that was hanging on the wall. He exited into a short tunnel that lead to the control room.

The General was waiting for him.

"Well, what do you think?"

"It's not what I think, but what I know. And right now I can't be sure. Something is wrong."

"For a while there it didn't look like there was any conversation at all. You and the girl were just staring at each other."

"It would seem that we were speaking to each other with our minds."

The General's eyes remained steady, he didn't move an inch, or show any sign of emotion. "That's something that can't be proved now, can it?"

"It seemed real. But no, I can't prove it. I can't explain it either. I have been hypnotized a few times in the past, to test its validity, so I know what that is like, and this could very well be such a case. I can't prove that I was conversing with her. But it seemed real."

Nick stopped speaking and stared through the window at Reva for a moment before continuing.

"But now she will attempt to transport me from outside this facility back to where she is."

Now both men were staring at Reva whose face was tilted to the side as though she were listening in on their conversation.

"General, I'll need three high speed cameras filming me on the outside, just in case this actually happens. One of the cameras must be infrared. And I want the same set-up filming that room."

"We have that equipment, and we can feed it into the control room."

"On the one hand I don't believe for a moment this is even remotely possible. And yet on the other hand I don't want to take any chances."

"I don't either. Taking chances can get you killed. This is not a problem, we can monitor the feed from inside here."

"Good, then let's move."

The General barked out orders to his aides in the control room and within a few short minutes six soldiers were at his side with cameras and tripods and were checking their controls.

"Wireless," said the General. Three of the soldiers with cameras exited the room with Nick. The other three began to set up their cameras in front of the mirrored window.

"I'll wait inside," said the General. "And keep my

eyes on our alien."

While the lights in the interior of the control room were red, the lights in the exit chamber were very dim red, so that when they walked through the door to the outside, their eyes were well adjusted to the night.

"Where should we set up the cameras?" asked Nick.

"Anywhere you want sir," replied the soldier. "This is your show."

Nick hesitated for a moment at those words. "Right," he said finally. This *was* like a show. He just hoped it didn't turn out to be a comedy with him as the stooge. Or a tragedy with someone getting hurt.

22.

Even though there was no moon, there were also no clouds, and in the clear mountain air, the stars lit up the sky. The milky way galaxy stretched overhead with its hundreds of billions of stars lighting their way.

The ground was uneven and rocky, and Nick began walking with his camera crew following, one of them had a noticeable limp, but Nick didn't ask about it and kept walking until they were well over two hundred yards from the command center. He turned back to look at the outline of the center's shadow.

"This should be far enough," he said.

Far enough for nothing at all to happen, he thought to himself.

The three cameramen spread out equal distance around Nick, set up the tripods, securing the legs, powering up their equipment, focusing the lenses, and checking the wireless connections to the command center.

Each in turn gave a thumbs up. "We're all connected and ready when you are sir."

Ready for a pie in the face, thought Nick with a frown. Here goes nothing. Should I close my eyes like I'm praying, or keep them open and watch towards the tent? What's the protocol? She didn't tell him exactly what to do.

He sat down on the hard ground, folded his legs for comfort and stability, and wrapped his forearms around his knees, locking his fingers to keep his posture solid.

I'm keeping my eyes open, he decided and focused on the approximate area where he thought Bob and Reva were located.

A light wind was gently blowing across the mountain, ruffling the hair above his ears. In the quiet he could hear his heartbeat.

He projected his thoughts towards the tent. 'I'm here, and I'm ready.'

Nothing happened.

Maybe I'm not trying hard enough, he thought. Or maybe this is where the enemies he'd made throughout his life got their revenge. Filming him sitting on the ground like a buffoon waiting to beamed up by an alien, and laughing on the sidelines.

What did Reva say? Calm your mind. Remove all thoughts and anxiety. Concentrate on one thing and one thing only with all your heart, the single space where she was located, reach out and feel for her.

Within the space of half a breath, he felt the presence of Reva as though she were standing right next to him, startled, he looked around and only saw the cameras surrounding him, the camera men with questioning anxious faces, one eye on the cameras to make sure they were operating, and one eye on him.

"I'm here," he heard in his mind, a resonating sound bypassing his ears straight to his cortex. Not really words, but a symphony. His eyes instinctively closed and blackness surrounded him. He felt a pressure on the center of his forehead as though a soft balloon was being pressed against it, then enveloping his entire body. He was both inside the balloon, and it was pressing outward from every inch inside of him.

The overarching, encompassing feeling that he'd always carried within but never realized was there until it was suddenly going away, began shedding off him like water off a pane of glass, fear of loss, fear of the past, the future, the present, his ever present overwhelming ego, pity, shame, superiority, self-worth, all sliding away and revealing something that he did not know was hidden at the center of his core, his being, shining with a light beyond light.

"I'm here," he thought with a joy that he'd never experienced. "And I've always been here."

Reva's thoughts greeted him with something between a command and a request, gentle yet firm. "Now come here."

He had a sudden feeling like he was floating in air, no gravity, no air pressure, no body; like he was shot out of a cannon. With a sudden burst of acceleration and blinding light, the soft balloon that both pressed against him and enveloped him cushioning the crushing speed of him leaving one pinpoint in time and space to another. And yet he was at once both in the place he'd left and at the place he was going, while being in the middle as well. Surrounded by infinity, enveloped by it, becoming a part of it.

He wanted to scream but had no voice, the sudden terror of transporting through space was quickly overwhelmed by a golden light that enveloped him and carried him through a wall of time and space and deposited him with a loud 'pop' next to Reva.

She was holding out her hands and clutching his tightly while he sat heavily on the ground. Through a fog he could see her calm face and black eyes, and yet still felt the presence of her mind within his. She was calming him, soothing him with a voice like a song.

A breath came into his lungs, shallow and steep as though he'd never breathed before. As though he'd never been alive before this very moment. He could hear the air hissing through his clenched teeth and down along his tight throat into his scorched chest, then exhaled and brought another quick breath to replace it lest he be unable to breathe again. He felt every inch of skin and every bone in his body and let out a sigh.

His head felt light and he knew he was about to pass out. He tried to fight it, to stay conscious.

Less than a moment ago he was outside in the

chilled dark night air and now he was inside a brightly lit enclosure.

In the space of a split second his mind whirled and he deciphered what had just happened. Not less than a moment ago… he stopped that thought, it wasn't a separate moment, it was the same moment, connected by the gel that holds everything in the entire universe together.

He blinked once, then lost consciousness.

23.

The three camera men with their top-of-the-line video equipment trained on Nicholas Gold, were part of the Primary Military Occupational Specialty whose acronym was: PMOS 4641.

The duties of their particular squad in the United States Marine Corps was to calmly and competently take digital photographs and videos in both peacetime and the turbulence of war, in a wide range of environments including darkness, underwater, or under hostile enemy fire, to be used for civil affairs, intelligence gathering, recruiting, investigations, field research and historical records.

None of them were told ahead of time what it was they were recording, and none of them had any idea about what, if anything, was about to happen.

It was a simple order: follow the subject wherever he wanted to go, then film him from three separate and equal angles. They were not to interact with the subject in any way, shape, or form. Do not assist him or restrict him and stay out of his way.

It was a simple order and even though they were

photographers whose basic inclination was in looking for unusual and creative shots, as soldiers, they were ready willing and able to carry out the simple direct order:

Set up your cameras and stay out of the way.

One of them was a new recruit with a degree from a top-notch photography institute, had just gotten out of boot camp, and this was his first real assignment, while the other two had already been in actual combat with people shooting guns and mortars at them.

Of those two, one was wounded, shot in the leg and received the purple heart, while the other received an award for a photo he took of a Marine rescuing a young boy from a bombed-out building.

All three saw Nicholas Gold disappear.

It happened so suddenly, with no warning, that for a moment they weren't even sure what, if anything, they had seen.

Their cameras were all operational. The red blinking lights on the screens showed that the cameras were recording. All three were hooked to the wireless system and the video feeds were going straight to the central command post a few hundred yards away. All three had two back-up systems each, one was a separate hard drive mounted below the camera, and the other an internal hard drive. Nothing was left to chance.

All was calm and quiet. Their subject was in the middle of a circle of the three wide angle lenses, positioned less than ten feet away. There were two video cameras and one infrared camera all with high speed thousand frame per second capability. They could catch a bullet in flight and show it like a snail crawling across the screen to its target.

A single light array that was attached to one of the video cameras lit the subject perfectly. Nick was sitting on the ground with his eyes open, facing the command center.

Seconds and minutes passed by and nothing happened. The photographers looked uneasily at each other now and again, while keeping their attention on their equipment to make sure that they were still recording.

Their subject still had his eyes open, he even looked around at them for moment with a strange perplexed look of fear or anxiety before closing his eyelids, becoming perfectly calm. He even seemed to stopped breathing.

No warning.

The loud POP jolted all three of them, jumping involuntarily as though someone had fired a gun, as they watched the clothes that Nick wore slowly crumple to the ground. A small cloud of dust swirled in the spot where Nick had been, displaced by the sudden vacuum of a large man that was now gone.

None of them made a sound. Not a word, not a peep came out of their mouths.

Stunned to silence, barely breathing, they looked with furtive glances at each other to see the reactions on each of their faces, not believing what they had just seen, then quickly back to their cameras to make certain that the red recording symbol was still blinking.

After that, none of them moved a muscle, or attempted to touch the cameras for fear of losing some sort of footage.

The Marine photographer who'd been shot in combat had a walkie talkie on his belt, but he was afraid to touch it for fear that the radio signal might interfere with the video signals going to the command center.

He wanted to call in to his commander to report what they'd seen and ask for orders, but all of his appendages were numb, he was in shock and couldn't move his arm to bring the radio up to his face.

Their subject was gone and maybe they should just wait until someone from the command tent came to get them.

24.

"By God that's the most amazing thing I've ever seen," shouted the General. His face was a bright ruddy red from the excitement as he paced back and forth in front of Nick. "What was it like? How did it feel?"

Nick was still in shock. When he woke up on the floor next to Reva, his mind was like a drifting white cloud in an endless blue sky. His body felt like a puddle of jelly and he couldn't move for a few long moments. His entire being was exhausted as though he'd run ten consecutive marathons, then been crushed by a house-sized boulder, pulled along the bottom of the ocean, then flopped out and hung to dry on a clothesline.

It took five guards to carry him naked out of the quarantine room, put him through the sterilization procedure, dress him and set him in the chair in the command center.

His senses began to come back to him, and he shook his head in amazement. He'd travelled through time and space in a split second and he remembered it as though it was an eternity, since in essence it was.

He knew now that *everything* was eternity, the here and the now, the past and the future, all rolled into one ever-existing all-encompassing moment.

The General stopped his pacing and stood in front of Nick, waiting for an answer.

Nick blinked his eyes, like a fighter on the wrong side of a knock-out punch.

"What did you say?"

"I asked you what it was like and how it felt to be transported."

He blinked his eyes again. The no-nonsense ironclad General believed that he had transported.

"Here, take a look at this."

Nick was wheeled over to the front of a computer screen. The General scrolled a mouse and the screen lit up, it was a split screen with three side-by-side images on top, and three on the bottom. At the top right of each image was a time stamp in hours, seconds, and milliseconds.

"The top is you out in the field, and bottom is the room with our detainees. As you can see, all the images are time matched. Watch this."

He pressed the start button, the numbers started changing like a blur on the millisecond box. On the screen, Nick could see his face turn to his right, seemingly startled, then seemed to calm down, take a deep breath, and suddenly disappear, while instantaneously on the bottom screen he appeared, holding onto Revas hands before slumping to the floor in heap.

The skeptic in Nick tried to rise within him but withered as he remembered the feeling of instant acceleration, and something else that lingered within him. A glimpse of creation.

"Now watch this," said the General and scrolled the footage back to when Nick was still out in the field, then brought it forward to the single frame where he disappeared and scrolled back and forth between them a couple of times.

"One thousand frames per second. In one frame you're in the field and in the next you're in the room." He clicked on one of the top frames and increased the magnification until the image of him sitting there filled the screen, then clicked forward one frame, then back, over and over.

Nick leaned forward, intrigued. This was the moment that he transported. There in one thousandth of a second, gone the next. The scientist inside of him returned. He brought his face closer to the screen, then turned to the General and reached for the mouse. "Do you mind if I take over for a moment?"

The General shook his head and took a step back to give him room.

He took over the mouse and increased the magnification even further until his whole head filled the screen. He clicked forward to the frame where he had disappeared and then forward a few more frames. There was some sort of disturbance in the air. A slight wisp of condensation outlining the shape of his head and collapsing to the center of the sudden void. It was nearly imperceptible.

"What is it?" asked the General.

"Air filling a vacuum at the speed of sound. The condensation that you see is the same effect that you have on the front of a supersonic aircraft as it breaks through the sound barrier."

Nick scrolled the mouse again until there three frames apiece in the split screen and picked an image on the bottom, where he appeared in the room, and increased the magnification again until his head filled the screen. In one frame he wasn't there, and the next, he was.

There, imperceptibly at the edges of his face and hair, was the condensation in reverse, not collapsing into the void, but expelled in a mini shock wave.

"This is the popping sound," said Nick. "When an object is transported."

Intrigued he clicked onto the infrared sequence when he was in the field and scrolled to the point where he disappeared and increased the magnification. There was a very faint outline of his head in the first frame when he had disappeared; a red tinged heat signature that turned white as it collapsed.

"What is it?" asked the General. "Some sort of radiation?"

"No. It's the air that surrounded my head before I disappeared. A thin layer of atmospheric gas that was heated by my body temperature, the infrared camera senses it the microsecond after I disappear. You'll notice the area right in front of my nose, like a geyser of heat. I must have been breathing out at that exact moment."

He moussed over and pulled up the infrared sequence in the quarantine room, magnified it until his head filled the screen and scrolled to the frame right before he appeared. There was zero heat signature, and then in the proceeding frames, a halo of red heat surrounded his head and was expelled outward in a swirling cloud that disappeared a few inches away from him.

"A gas, such as our atmosphere, expelled from a void at the speed of sound will heat with friction as the molecules crash against each other. This is what we're seeing here."

"These cameras," said the General, "record at one thousand frames per second, but that's obviously not fast enough. We're not seeing the exact moment that you disappear. The next time we do this, we'll need a faster camera. I want to see the frame that shows the transition."

Nick thought back to the precise instant that he transported, less than twenty minutes ago. The memory was fresh in his mind.

"I don't think it's possible," said Nick, "for a camera to record that moment in time, if you can even call it that; as though you are separating something that is not separate. Somehow, someway, I'm certain that time is a continuous loop. The shortest measurable amount of time in theory is called Planck time."

"How short is that?"

"If our cameras are recording at one thousandth of a second, that is a 'one' followed by three zeros. A Planck is a 'one' followed by forty-four zeros. There are more Planck increments in a single second than all the seconds since the big bang thirteen point seven billion years ago."

The General furrowed his brow, squinting his eyes and trying to fathom that fraction.

"But that's not necessarily the shortest *increment* of time," continued Nick. "For that we have to look at quantum gravity physics…"

"Let's get to the point," said the General, agitated.

"I can't explain it," said Nick, silent for a moment as his eyes drifted back to the screen with the infrared halo of air frozen in an image of time. "But I've been there. I believe now that time is infinite, both small and large. There is no end of time either way you go. There is no end and no beginning, it is one continuous, ever-present now. I'll never be able to explain it, even to myself, but in that moment that I transported, time was infinite both in the smallest amount and the largest, as though forever and nothing were merged into one."

"You're babbling," said the General. "Settle yourself and let's get to the point."

"I've never been more coherent in my life," said Nick with a sigh. "They're from another planet, alright. It's finally happened, what we've all been waiting for, only it didn't happen like everyone thought it would. They didn't travel in a flying saucer through a wormhole in space. They didn't travel in any vehicle at all. They travelled with a single thought. A single, pure thought. And they're not little green men, or toad-like creatures, or thinking blobs. They're just like us. Only they're probably better than us, more refined, more thoughtful and kind."

Nick was silent again as it all sank in. He was finally face-to-face with an alien creature, an entire alien race, and he was suddenly somehow completely enraptured with it.

The general nodded.

"I was afraid of that. Actually."

His voice drifted off and he gazed at Bob and Reva through the plexiglass, then pulled himself together, took a deep breath and turned towards his assistant, who stood nearby, waiting.

With a stone cold face he gave the order.

"Pull out a hundred of the strongest looking ones, half male, half female, and bring them up to the holding area. Do it quickly."

Nick's eyes narrowed. They were separating the population.

"What about the rest of them General? What about the other hundred thousand beings down there?"

The old man turned and looked at Nick with calm, dead eyes, and while his lips said nothing, the eyes said it all. Nick couldn't read the General's mind, but he knew exactly what was going on behind those lifeless eyes.

Nick shook his head, the horror building in his gut. "You can't be thinking of eliminating the rest of them."

The general remained silent.

"You bastard," said Nick. "You're going to cull the herd. Who gave you the right?"

"Sometimes hard decisions need to be made. I would drop the bomb on an enemy nation full of humans if they threatened our country's survival, you don't think I'd drop it on an alien invasion?"

"Those are sentient beings out there huddled together. They need our help. For God's sake, they're nearly human."

"But they're not human," said the General. "Are they? And that's the ultimate problem that we are facing, wouldn't you say? One of them has already mated with a human, and we don't know how that will turn out. A hybrid, a mutation, something from which there is no turning back."

"What if it's something wonderful?"

"That's a chance we can't afford to take."

"You're talking genocide."

"I'm talking survival!" the General shouted, pounding his hand on the table, purple veins popping out on the side of his neck. "If any one of them ever gets out into our population, it'll be end of the human race as we know it."

"Right about now I'm thinking that might not be a bad thing."

"That's why you're not in charge. They're not human."

"Are you?"

"Survival is the most basic human trait."

"I thought it was compassion. You heard her. They're all that's left from their planet."

"So she says. How do we know if she's telling the truth, take her at her word? You would trust the survival of the entire human race, maybe all the life on this planet with a statement from an alien? And you think I lack compassion? What about the compassion for all the other life on this planet? What about your friends and your family? Don't they deserve the courtesy of us finding out just exactly what we're up against, before it's too late? We'll allow a few of them to continue living, but we can't accommodate all of them. Not here, not now. Maybe sometime in the future, when we know more about them, we could allow their population to increase, but for now we need to keep it small and controllable. And very, very secret."

"You'll study them."

The General nodded, the popping veins gone, calm and calculating again. "Yes."

Nick knew what that entailed. They would be subjected to all types of intrusive testing, including cutting them up into little bits to look at the inner workings of their brains and bodies, vivisection while still alive. They would also be tortured in some ways: electric shock, air deprivation, pressure chambers, centrifugal force, mental, physical.

"Does the President know about this?"

"This isn't in his job description."

"You'll use them for the military."

"Of course. Can you imagine the potential?"

Nick knew where this was leading.

The general continued. "We'll nurture them and develop them. We can have a mind reading spy in every communication center of our adversaries. With a single one of them behind enemy lines we can transport an entire army with a thought."

The General was silent for a moment as he processed that vision. Then he snapped his fingers.

"Hell, we wouldn't even need an army behind enemy lines. All we would really need is one assassin. Transport him into a room with whatever Premier or President or King is on the other side of us, and bang. End of conflict."

Nick looked at the general and realized what pure evil looked like. "You're sick. All you want is to develop them into a weapon to control and destroy."

"We'll need you on our team Nick," said the General, his hope fading as he studied the facial and body language of the man across from him.

"Over my dead body," said Nick as he jumped up and sprinted for the door. He didn't get very far.

The General motioned with his hand and the two sentries standing at the exit tried to tackle Nick, one high and one low.

Nick's martial arts training came into play, ducking and weaving as he gave a high karate kick to the jaw of the first sentry, and a short downwards punch to the temple on the side of the head of the second, and they both tumbled past him.

Then, five more sentries piled through the doorway, the first one, also trained in the arts, ducked a punch and rammed the butt of his rifle up into Nick's solar plexus, knocking the wind out of him.

Suddenly, all five of the sentries had their hands on him, lifting, turning, then pile-driving him into the ground. A combined thousand pounds of grunt. They quickly zip tied his hands and feet, while the biggest one sat on his back

"I have to warn them," whispered Nick as he kicked his feet in vain while his head was shoved into the floor.

With one eye he could see the General walk slowly forward and stand towering over him, his face devoid of compassion.

"The plane is in the air."

25.

Commander Ellis Campbell felt the slight vibration from the last bit of contact with the asphalt as the aircraft lifted off the tarmac at two hundred miles per hour. There were a couple more bumps as the hydraulics lifted the wheels into their sealed compartments, then all became smooth wind on metal, untethered by the bounds of earth.

Pulling back on the flight stick with one hand, while hitting the throttle with the other, he went up at a thirty-five-degree angle, g-forces pushing him down into his seat. He wanted to yell into his oxygen mask, the thrill of acceleration overwhelming him.

He was flying, the exhilaration and total commitment to speed and control never ceased to amaze him. He concentrated on the task at hand, which was to ride this bad boy straight into the night sky.

He learned early on in his career to tamp down the enthusiasm that naturally occurred in a human being as they broke the chains of gravity and hurtled into space in any type of vehicle, whether it was a pogo stick or a swing set on the playground outside the kindergarten classroom. And here he was, piloting a hundred-million-dollar machine, courtesy of the US Government. He eased the throttle forward and barreled into the sky, increasing the speed of the F-35 Lighting II quickly to five hundred miles per hour with the most powerful jet engine in the world.

The maximum speed of the aircraft he was riding in was twelve hundred miles per hour with a ceiling of fifty thousand feet, but he would need neither with the mission he was assigned to tonight.

He leveled out at twenty-five thousand feet, banked to the left, and headed for the Sierra Nevada mountains. Destination: The Marine Corps Mountain Training facility to deliver two five-hundred-pound laser guided thermal bombs to a target the size of five football fields.

It was a training run, he got the call during the morning briefing at three AM over a cup of coffee in the ward room surrounded by other pilots and officers. A live fire drill, and when he heard those two words, live fire, his heart rate jumped with both fear and joy, but on the outside he was cool as a cucumber, no emotion.

"Commander Campbell, you're on the hot seat for this bombing run, are you ready?"

"Yes sir," was his steady reply.

They always made the training runs out to be like a real life experience with real people in the mix and came up with scenarios to give it authenticity, otherwise it would seem too routine, training runs needed to have a sense of urgency and purpose, or the pilots and ground crew lost interest, so it was a game in itself to provide a believable back story line.

On the large wall was broadcast the finely detailed topographic image of the Sierra mountain range with a white square rectangle outlining the target area.

The man in charge with the pointer began.

"Gentlemen, this is our battle area. We have a company of US Marines pinned down on the flank of this mountain, who are unable to extricate themselves and are taking on extensive casualties. The enemy is raining mortars, RPG's, and machine gun fire from their high point here at the top edge of this box. Our mission is to provide immediate close air support and deliver a pinpoint air strike."

He looked directly at Ellis.

"You, Commander Campbell will take off immediately and follow a flight path to this location east of the target, and when you are in position you'll be given the command to deliver the ordinance. Our troops are in close proximity to the enemy and that is why we have chosen your aircraft as the delivery system. We have a spotter on the ground who will light the enemy controlled area with an encrypted laser. When you have radar confirmation of the laser target, you'll begin your bombing run from twenty thousand feet, and complete it at ten thousand feet."

Training missions were important for any type of military personnel whether it was an infantry grunt manning or storming a fox hole, medical support, or even the driver of a supply vehicle to the front lines. It was no less so for a pilot whose job it was to drop a five-hundred-pound bomb on someone's head. No one in their right mind would actually *want* to drop a bomb on someone unless it was absolutely necessary and the lives of their friends were in danger. Even then, it was a brutal thing to do, especially with the types of conventional weapons they carried that could decimate a city block, let alone a nuclear weapon that could destroy an entire city.

Regardless of what was portrayed in the movies, if you ever had a speeding ticket or a DUI, or were ever bankrupt, defaulted on a loan, or arrested for a fight, you wouldn't get anywhere near the controls of a hundred-million-dollar-machine.

To get to the point where the military would give you possession of a mass casualty weapon you had to prove that you wouldn't turn it on the people around you, and that's why the extensive background checks, the mental and physical tests were intrusive and intensive, to make sure they didn't have a latent loony bin on their hands—or someone who would freeze up at the wrong time and not be able to deliver when it counted. That was one of the biggest unknown factors: how someone would actually react in a battle situation when it really was all on the line. That's why they trained constantly, to take the emotion out of the equation.

They trained in the classrooms, in simulators, and

with real aircraft in battle simulated drills with dummy warheads, over and over again. And then every once in a while they'd get the call out of the blue for a live fire drill, just to keep their edges sharp in case it was actually needed at some point in the future. Fighter pilots were highly trained, living, breathing, thinking pieces of machinery of military might.

Commander Ellis looked out the cockpit window at the black sky above him, then down at the barely visible ghost white sands of Death Valley, slipping past below him.

Airspeed eight hundred fifty miles per hours, altitude twenty-five thousand feet. The speed of sound being seven hundred fifty miles per hour, and since he was well above that and dragging the sound-breaking cone along behind him, anyone on the ground far below would hear what they might mistake for a gunshot and the slight roar of the afterburners long after the aircraft had passed.

Leaving Death Valley behind, he straddled the low-lying Inyo mountain range and followed it north, travelling the fifty-mile length of it in four minutes, then banked left twenty degrees, the g-forces increasing to two gravities, skirting Mono Lake on the left-wing tip and then straightened out aiming for White Mountain and the Marine Corps Mountain Training area.

He said a quick rosary: "Hail Mary full of grace, bless us now and at the hour of our death."

Five minutes to the target. Time to rock and roll. He flipped the switch on a monitor and music trickled into his head set. Heavy metal, slash and burn bass guitar and drums pounding out a vicious tune, just like the bombs he was about to unleash.

He lowered his airspeed to under eight hundred, under seven hundred, under six hundred, and at five hundred and fifty knots he pushed the stick down and began the descent for the bombing run.

Two minutes to target.

The first lines of mountains were rising fast towards him. Radar engaged, the screen on his right showed the bullseye ten miles out, now five. He made the sign of the cross and with one push of a button, the small doors under the fuselage opened. Then he pressed the button releasing the bombs from their bays and watched on the screen as they headed towards their destination, guided by the infrared light of the laser lighting up the target, a green glow on the screen as the cameras on the front of the bombs recorded the image in high definition. He banked hard to the right away from the target, evasive maneuver to escape a potential ground to air missile and hit the afterburner to get the aircraft up into the six hundred mile per hour range, He then banked sharply up and away from the danger zone, and yet, on his screen he followed the two bombs to their impact zone one mile away, closing the distance in ten seconds time in slow motion. It was going straight down and into some sort of mass that was spread out on the side of the mountain, straight down into a sudden crowd of uplifted faces and then blankness. He cringed suddenly at the image that disintegrated in the explosion.

"What the hell was that!" he whisper-yelled, his heart jumping out of his throat and his eyes blinking wildly trying to erase the vision from his mind which instinctively knew that something was wrong.

He nearly lost control of the jet as his hand involuntarily jerked at the controls, he saw clearly in the blink of an eye the bombs barreling into the side of the mountain and a vast crowd of faces.

People.

Dear God.

He rolled out of the turn, struggling to maintain control of the jet climbing at a forty-five-degree angle, then leveled out at fifteen thousand feet. He headed straight east, away from the mountain range, and fought to catch his breath.

His heart was trying to beat its way out of his chest, the thumping sound drowning out the heavy metal music which was still in his head set. With a quick flip, he turned off the music and listened to the steady roar of the jet engine and the six hundred mile-per-hour wind on the canopy while looking straight up at the heavens and wondering what just happened.

Then he laughed nervously. It was a test.

That's all, just a test. They set up a few hundred dummies in the center of the impact zone to see how the munitions would impact them, and maybe to see how he would react when he saw the image as the bombs reached their deadly target.

"They were just dummies," he murmured, and smiled at the camera which was recording all his moves in the cockpit and would be analyzed by the support team, like a football team analyzing the tape of the big game. The visor on his helmet was mirrored and they wouldn't be able to see the trembling fear in his eyes in that single split second when he thought the dummies were real people. He flipped the switch on the microphone and his voice transmitted over an encrypted radio signal.

He tried to speak but no words came out, his throat dry as the desert below, and then he steadied himself.

"Bobcat one to base, over."

"Roger, loud and clear."

"Mission accomplished. Heading home."

"Roger that Bobcat. Over and out."

Just a bunch of very real looking dummies, thought Commander Ellis again. But in the back of his mind there was a gathering dark cloud, a creeping cold dread that maybe they were real people. He had no facts to base it on, but he still couldn't shake it. He also knew that in that instant he had to quickly come to grips with the fact that he wasn't cut out to drop bombs on people after all.

There was no way around it.

He was a sensible man.

The government gave him control of this fast-moving jet, this killing machine, because he could think quickly and react under strenuous circumstances with composure. And yet, one thing in his mind was now clear as the sky above him, he would never fly this plane again.

Maybe I can fly troop transports, or supply aircraft, he thought. *Or maybe I can go back to civilian life, driving big rig trucks, that was fun.* He smiled at that idea, driving all around the country in a big rig. Maybe get a floppy-eared hound dog to ride shotgun, hanging its head out the open window as they cruised down the open highway in the country.

And then the vision of the exploding crowd of faces came rushing back into his mind and he shuddered. The cold dread returning with a shiver down the back of his neck.

The first thing I have to do, he thought while steadying his shaking hands. *Is land this plane without crashing.*

26.

The hermetically sealed door opened and two of the guards threw Nick through the entrance and back into the quarantine tent with Bob and Reva. His arms and legs shackled and hogtied, he tried to maneuver his way to a chair, but gave up and just laid there with his head tilted onto the floor.

They saw the flash of light through the cracks in the windows and felt the earth tremble with the blast, the walls of the tent flexing with the shock wave. The sound of the explosion rolled over them for nearly a minute and then faded away, echoing off into the mountains and ravines and hills in the distance.

Reva put her hands over her face and quietly sobbed for a moment, then gathered herself and was silent. She wiped the tears from the corners of her eyes and reached with her mind outside of the tent, to the dead and those still dying.

It was over. They'd travelled six hundred light years and escaped their planet's destruction by a supernova only to be destroyed by the hands of man.

Bob was looking down at Nick, and slowly shook

his head. His face was blank, unable to hide the disgust in his heart.

"I'm a prisoner now, just like you," said Nick. "You have to know that none of this was my doing. I tried to stop them."

Nick closed his eyes for a moment thinking about the thousands of beings on the plateau, and when he opened them again Bob was still staring down at him. "I have a feeling that you and I and Reva will never get out of here and no one will ever know what happened up here on this mountain."

"What does it matter now?" said Bob.

"I'm as ashamed as you are."

"Ashamed of what?"

"To be human."

"How do you know we ever were?" said Bob. "Maybe we're all just monsters with human masks."

"Don't try to lump me in with those people out there."

"Why not? What makes you think that you or me or anyone else on this planet is anything special."

"It's too kind to compare us to monsters."

Nick rotated his head on the ground and looked over at Reva. Now that they had been connected through inter-mind conversation and an interpersonal transportation, they would always be connected. He reached out with his mind to her, reached out with his mind so that no one behind the glass could hear what he was about to ask.

What about the two that went over the ridge?

Her eyes had a look of desperation in them, cobalt black and hardened, while her mind was silent. Then slowly, the edges of her eyes softened, and he knew without a word spoken or unspoken what she was thinking.

They were safe.

27.

The old woman was ninety-one years old and lived alone in a small one-story stone and mortar house near the mountain.

Built by her husband with his own two hands in the middle of the last century when they were young newlyweds with few cares in the world, she'd lived there nearly all her life, raising a family of five children, then watching as they slowly left her one by one. Her husband had passed ten years ago, and her children had all, long before that, moved away to live their own lives with their own families. Now, she was all alone.

She never remarried, at her old age what good would come of it? She was too set in her ways to adjust to the nuances of anyone else in the house with her and decided to live out the rest of her days with her memories.

The children worried about her and every now and then pleaded with her to move down to the city where they could see her and take care of her, but what they really wanted was for her to move into an old folks' home, so they wouldn't have to worry about her at all. They wanted to live their lives without a nagging feeling in the back of their minds that they were neglecting their poor old mom.

"Fiddlesticks," she muttered, plainly stating to the empty walls: "I've lived this long on my own, and I'm fairly certain I can live a whole lot longer by my own strength and wits."

Stubborn as she was, though, little things were getting tougher for her to accomplish.

Bending over to feed the cat was a chore, opening a can to make a cup of soup for herself took a tremendous effort. One day she couldn't manage to get one of the windows open for some fresh air, and just left it closed and went outside to sit on the porch instead.

Summer was ending, the warm air slowly eroding with the shortening of the days, the nights becoming colder, nipping at her grisled skin. Soon the leaves on all the trees, except for the pines and the evergreens, would turn gold and drop. Then the snow would come, and with it, the bitter cold. But for now the weather was pleasant and warm.

One day while sitting on the rocking chair on the front porch she saw a young man approach from the road. He was barefoot and wearing only a grey towel that was tucked around his waist and extended down to his knees. His skin was smooth with a reddish-brown tint, his hair black and straight, and his eyes were black like hardened coal with a gentle and kind demeanor.

He waved to her and without a second thought she lifted an old crooked arthritic hand and waved back.

There was something about that young man that was odd, and yet nonthreatening. She felt a strange feeling in her heart when she looked at him, and his eyes did not waver from hers as he strolled by the house.

"Come up here," she said with as loud a voice as she could muster at her old age. "So I can see you better." He walked slowly up to the edge of the porch.

"What are you doing here?" she asked with suspicion.

He didn't say anything at first and just looked at her with his kind, searching eyes. Then she felt, more than heard, him say, *I'm travelling down the road.*

She squinted hard at his face in the fading light. Her eyes were old after all and it was hard enough to see clearly in the full light of day, let alone near sunset.

Did his lips move while he spoke? She couldn't tell and asked him to repeat himself.

"So you're traveling down the road are you?"

He pointed to the side at the asphalt pavement and again she felt the words:

I'm travelling down the road.

This time she watched carefully, and was certain that his lips did not move, but for some strange reason it didn't seem to matter anymore.

"Yes, I can clearly see that," she said. An

overwhelming sense of empathy swept over her and she felt a sudden glow in her heart for him.

The feelings that she abruptly felt and that came rushing back to her, she knew without even thinking, were the same that she felt when her babies were small and needed her. The feelings that a mother has for her children. Feelings that no one in history has ever been able to completely describe with words.

They stared at each other for a moment that stretched off in time, and then she knew what needed to be done.

"I could use some help around here," she said. "If you're looking for work. I can't pay you much, but you can have a place to rest, and food to eat."

I will take care of you, she thought silently to herself. *And keep you safe from harm.*

She watched him carefully for a response, but he only stared at her with those eyes. Then the old woman heard the thought from him in her mind:

I'd like that.

He turned around and motioned behind him towards the woods where a young girl with long black hair down past her waist came walking out. She was dressed in a long, colorful silk wrap that she held close with her arms wrapped around her shoulders. Beautiful coal black eyes and bare feet.

Can my sister join me?

Something stirred deep within her breast, and the old woman's heart was nearly overwhelmed, then she smiled. "Why yes, of course."

She straightened herself in the chair while looking down at the two of them. "You know, there are plenty of other young folk around this area just about your age. I'll bet you could get to know them and be their friend."

They walked slowly up to the rickety porch steps hand in hand, vivid black eyes fixed on the old woman as she rose slowly to her feet, ligaments and bones creaking with the effort.

Then as she turned to open the front door for her guests, she wasn't quite certain what she actually heard, for it was like in a dream that her ears caught the soft rolling physical sound of the word as they said it in unison:

"Namalamanse."

It was as clear in her mind as though a melody was being projected from an orchestra in heaven. It was resonating and bouncing throughout the depths of her heart, every fiber, every nerve ending, every synapse of her old body was transformed into a brand-new gleaming harpsichord, a living vibrating musical instrument, and she *felt* the word:

Friend.